CRASH!

This was her chance! Kiki raced to the entry hall and turned toward the open doorway of Jeffrey's room.

"There she is!" one of the men yelled.

The beam of the flashlight flared on her momentarily as he ran toward her and lunged at the door. Kiki was too fast for him but, luckily, not for Pumpkin. He catapulted into the room just as she slammed the door in the man's face and turned the lock. Her breath was coming in short gasps and her knees felt rubbery. She wanted to sit down, but she couldn't let down her guard now. What if they tried to break the door down? She glanced quickly around the room. There was a three-drawer chest up against one wall. She shoved it over in front of the door, tipped it on its side with a loud crash, and piled a chair and a small table on top. Pumpkin leaped to the summit of the furniture mountain and snarled.

"THIEF!"
SAID THE CAT

Louise
Munro Foley

A BERKLEY / SPLASH BOOK

"THIEF!" SAID THE CAT

A Berkley Book / published by arrangement with
General Licensing Company, Inc.

PRINTING HISTORY
Berkley edition / May 1992

A GLC BOOK

Splash is a trademark of General Licensing Company, Inc.

ISBN: 0-425-12732-X

A BERKLEY BOOK ® ™ 757,375
Berkley Books are published by The Berkley
Publishing Group, 200 Madison Avenue,
New York, New York 10016.
The name "BERKLEY" and the "B" logo
are trademarks belonging to Berkley Publishing Corporation.

PRINTED IN THE UNITED STATES OF AMERICA

10 9 8 7 6 5 4 3 2 1

With gratitude to
Jan Hood and Cathy Cole,
who made it happen

"THIEF!"

SAID THE CAT

Chapter One

"I'm leaving now, Kiki. Lock up when you go, and don't forget your keys."

Dr. Maryanne Collier's voice rose up the stairwell and brought Kiki back to the present with startling speed. She glanced at the clock. It was six-forty-five. She was due to babysit for the Kendricks at seven.

"And shut your window! They're forecasting rain."

"Okay, Mom." Kiki slid off the bed, dislodging the book that she'd been reading. It hit her foot and then the floor, and the large cat who'd been cozily curled up beside her growled his disgust at being disturbed. She hopped out to the landing, clutching her injured toes with one hand, and leaned over the railing.

"Bye, Mom!" The lanky redhead smiled down at the attractive woman in the lower hallway. "See you later." Kiki hopped on one foot and rubbed her sore toes.

Her mother looked at her quizzically. "Are you practicing for a three-legged race?"

"Dropped a book on my foot," Kiki replied, grimacing. "Limited coordination of the brain cells. Loosely translated, I'm a klutz. Will you be late?"

"I'm scheduled till midnight in emergency. If it's quiet, I'll be home by twelve-thirty . . . but you'd better be in bed by then! Mrs. Kendrick said they'd be home around ten. Be sure you put on the deadbolt!"

Her mother had been nervous about leaving her alone ever since two burglaries had occurred in the neighborhood in the last month, both almost as soon as the homeowner's car had left the driveway. It seemed as though the houses were being watched.

"Lighten up, Mom! I'm fourteen years old. I can look after myself!"

"Face it, Kiki: I'm your mother and I'll probably still be worrying about you when you're forty, so get used to it."

Dr. Collier waved and closed the door behind her. Kiki hopped back to her room, batting at the orange cat, who was finding this new game amusing. With each hop, the cat lunged at Kiki's suspended foot, threatening her balance and her patience.

"Cut it out, Pumpkin!" Kiki warned. She sat

2

down on the side of the bed and reached underneath for her tennis shoes. She pulled one out and wedged her foot into it. "Okay, what did you do with the other one?" The cat sat primly at her feet, gazing up with innocent green eyes as Kiki talked.

"Don't give me that I-don't-have-the-slightest-idea-what-you're-talking-about look, Pumpkin! You have two loves, chocolate and shoes. Shoes are one of your dog tricks, remember?"

The big cat meowed once and listened attentively.

"You hide shoes, and you chew on shoes, and you destroy shoes. Dirty shoes, clean shoes, old shoes, new shoes, dress shoes, gym shoes . . ." Kiki's singsong voice became more and more muffled as she crawled farther and farther under the bed to retrieve her missing footwear. When she backed out, with a couple of cat-fur dustballs clinging to her hair, Pumpkin was still sitting imperiously beside the bed, gazing at her.

"Enough of the injured-monarch look," Kiki said, tying the second shoe. "I've got to go. Try to stay out of trouble, okay?" She ruffled the cat's fur one last time, grabbed her backpack from under the desk, and made a beeline for the door, with the cat close on her heels. "Oh no you don't!" she said. "I'm on to that trick!" In one fluid motion she eased herself out into the upstairs hall, pushing the cat back with one hand, and quickly shut the door. An outraged squeal followed her down the stairs as she let herself out the front door and securely locked the deadbolt behind her. She glanced at her watch as she stood under the porch light. It was five to seven. She'd make it. The Kendricks lived just down the block.

Kiki started to run. The wind whining through the giant oaks that lined the street reminded her of her mother's warning. *Rats! I forgot my bedroom window.* She glanced up at the dark sky. *No time to go back now,* she thought. *Maybe it won't rain until morning, anyhow.*

Eeeoooww!

Suddenly, a familiar screech came hurtling through the night.

"Kiki," she said to herself grimly, "there are *two* reasons to shut the windows—to keep rain out and to keep cats in. You blew it!"

Eeoow! It was almost a conversational tone as Pumpkin caught up and ran alongside her.

"You dumb cat," Kiki said, not breaking stride. "You know what this means. It's into the backpack and not a squeak out of you until the Kendricks have left."

Meeeooow, Pumpkin interrupted.

"I'm not through," Kiki said. "This is my first time babysitting here. The Kendricks are new in

4

the neighborhood. They don't know you're the friendliest cat on the block. You'd better behave!"

She turned in at the long, sweeping driveway that made a semicircle in front of the Kendricks' large house. As she approached the door she slowed her pace. Putting Pumpkin into her backpack without his approval was not one of her favorite activities, although it was called for with amazing regularity lately. The previous month he had followed her onto the school bus that was taking them on a field trip to the salmon hatchery. It had been some job keeping the cat away from the fish—her backpack had taken on a life of its own during the tour. Sometimes he followed her to the library where he liked to sit perched on top of the shelves and meow his approval or disapproval of her book selections. On occasion Pumpkin could be both still and quiet when he was wedged in with her books, but Kiki could not predict with any certainty when that would happen. She hoped this was one of those occasions.

She slipped the pack off and reached down to pick up her pet. But Pumpkin was too quick for her. He darted into the shrubbery at the side of the house and huddled up against the foundation.

"Pumpkin!" Kiki said in a loud whisper. "Get

over here! Right now!" She squatted down on her haunches by a rosebush and looked in with her green eyes at the cat, who was looking back at her. "Pumpkin!" she repeated sternly. From inside the house she could hear a clock chiming the hour. "I'm going to be late!"

She reached in to grab him and, without warning, the orange cat hissed at her. Startled, Kiki brought her hand back to her side. "What is it?" she whispered. Pumpkin hardly ever hissed at her. He seemed to want her complete attention.

Meeeooow. Pumpkin clawed at the dirt in the flower bed.

"What is it?" She flopped on the grass and inched her way under the rosebush. A thorn scratched at her neck, and when she reached up to push it away another raised a welt on her hand. "Come on," she pleaded in a dramatic change of tone. "Nice Pumpkin, good Pumpkin. Come to Kiki."

But Pumpkin wasn't going anywhere. Dim light from a small basement window outlined his activity as he rapidly and intently scratched at the dirt under the bush.

"I know," said Kiki wearily. "It's another dog act. You're a mean old dog and you're digging up a bone. I'm impressed."

Pumpkin shrieked. He stopped digging and

grabbed her hand between his front paws with surprising force. Deliberately, the cat pulled Kiki's hand toward him, pushing something up against her fingers. It was a key.

"What's a key doing in the flower bed?" Kiki said aloud, stuffing it into the pocket of her jeans. "Weird."

His job done, Pumpkin marched out and hopped into the backpack, waiting to be tucked in. Kiki closed the flap loosely over his head, walked to the front door, and rang the bell. *Now be quiet,* she prayed silently as footsteps approached from inside. As if he could read her thoughts, Pumpkin shifted in the bag but made no noise.

Mr. Kendrick opened the door. "Hi, Kiki!" he said. "Come in! Brought your homework with you, I see. Just put your stuff down over there." He motioned to the living room. Luxurious lemon-colored carpet stretched from wall to wall. Kiki hesitated, mentally picturing the orange cat in her bag. He couldn't have escaped from his digging foray without getting dirty.

"Right here is fine," said Kiki, setting the pack down in the tiled entry hall beside a briefcase. "Sorry I'm late."

"You're not late," said Mr. Kendrick. "Susan is getting Jeffrey ready for bed. He's been looking forward to seeing you again."

The week before, just a few days after the Kendricks had moved in, Mrs. Kendrick had called Kiki and asked her to come and visit. She said Kiki had been recommended as a good babysitter and she wanted to meet her. So Kiki had stopped by on her way home from school the following day and met Mrs. Kendrick and Jeffrey, who was an okay kid as two-year-olds go. But this was the first time she had met Mr. Kendrick. He was as tall and dark as Mrs. Kendrick was short and blonde, and Kiki would have felt intimidated except for his lopsided grin. He was a friendly man with a quiet voice who looked more like a football player than the new county district attorney.

"Come on into the kitchen," he said, starting down the hall.

Kiki glanced at her backpack, hesitated only briefly, then picked it up and followed him.

"Kiki's an interesting name. Is it a nickname, or short for something else?"

Kiki wrinkled her nose. "Kathryn Kristine."

"Both lovely names, but I like Kiki, too. It seems to suit you." Mr. Kendrick opened the refrigerator and looked back over his shoulder at her. "Glass of milk?" he offered. "I'm going to have one."

"Sure," said Kiki, suddenly self-conscious. "Thanks." She wanted to ask him why he said

8

the name Kiki suited her, but thought she might put him on the spot. She figured he was probably just being polite and making conversation, the way adults did.

"Who dubbed you Kiki?" Mr. Kendrick asked. "Your mom?"

Kiki swallowed. "No, my father." She blinked her eyes quickly and looked away, hoping the tears would not come.

"You lost your father, didn't you," Mr. Kendrick said kindly. It wasn't a question, but a statement.

Kiki nodded, afraid that if she spoke, her voice would betray her emotions. It had been two years, but even now any mention of her dad made her cry.

Mr. Kendrick stroked his chin and looked at her thoughtfully. "Your mom told me about the car accident," he said. "I wasn't prying. I just think that if we're going to be friends, we need to know something about each other. My own father died when I was seven. It was rough growing up with just one parent." He reached over and lifted the plastic dome from a cake dish on the counter. "Susan made chocolate cupcakes today," he said. "Want one?"

Kiki was about to answer when her backpack, which she'd propped against a stool at the counter, suddenly came alive. An orange ball of fur streaked like a comet from the bag, circled the kitchen once at top speed, leaped to a chair and then to the counter, and assumed the pose of a marble statue, about three inches from Mr. Kendrick's face—and about one inch from the chocolate cupcakes.

Kiki closed her eyes and sighed. "You said the magic word," she said from between clenched teeth. "Chocolate."

But Mr. Kendrick didn't hear her. He was doubled over, laughing so hard that he was making no noise. He pushed his rimless glasses up on his head and wiped the tears from his eyes.

"And who," he spluttered, "is this?"

"Meet Pumpkin," Kiki replied. "Pumpkin is my cat."

She made a quick assessment while she was talking. The cat's forepaws looked okay. There was no visible dirt and no leaves or twigs in his fur. She knew she should be thankful for small mercies. At least the uninvited guest was presentable. The little brat had done an admirable job of cleaning up while in seclusion, but she hated to think what her books looked like.

"Kitty!" said a small voice from the doorway. Jeffrey was standing there, fresh from the bathtub, ready for bed in his footed sleeper. Behind him stood Mrs. Kendrick, puzzling over this new addition.

"I'm really sorry," Kiki apologized quickly. "I shut him in my room when I left, but he got out through the window and came down the trellis, I guess, and followed me here. I can put him in the basement until you get back, if that's okay." She looked from one parent to the other. "I didn't have time to take him back. And then he made me late, anyway . . . oh, and I forgot to tell you, Pumpkin found this key in your flower bed." She pulled the key from her pocket and laid it on the counter.

While Kiki was talking Pumpkin had seized the opportunity to jump down from the counter and nuzzle Jeffrey, who responded with undivided attention.

Mr. Kendrick slipped his glasses back on the bridge of his nose and grinned at her. "As I was saying," he said, waving his hand toward the plate of cupcakes, "would you like to have a—"

"Don't say it!" Kiki warned. "Don't say c-h-o-c-o-l-a-t-e." She spelled out the word, and Pumpkin looked up at her questioningly. "He's crazy for it. It's his favorite food."

"I never heard of such a thing," said Mrs. Kendrick, smiling. "A cat who eats ch—I mean, c-h-o-c-o-l-a-t-e! Well, he came to the right place! I was just going to give Jeffrey a cupcake before bed. Your furry friend can have one, too." She handed one to Jeffrey, then put another on

11

the floor. "There you go . . . uh . . ." She looked over at Kiki.

"Pumpkin," Kiki said. "His name is Pumpkin."

"There you are, Pumpkin," Mrs. Kendrick said, stroking his fur. Pumpkin looked at her adoringly as he licked at the frosting. "And you don't have to put him in the basement, Kiki," she added. "He can stay up here and keep you company." She paused. "He is housebroken, isn't he?"

Kiki nodded. "Yes, but that was about as far as my civilizing attempts succeeded."

"Speaking of the basement," Mrs. Kendrick said to her husband, "I just remembered the load of clothes in the dryer."

"I'll fold them for you," Kiki volunteered. Even though it didn't seem necessary, she was eager to do something to make up for bringing along her uninvited pet.

"That wasn't a hint!" said Mrs. Kendrick.

"I didn't think it was," Kiki said, "but I don't mind folding clothes. I'll get them."

"Well, if you feel like it," said Mrs. Kendrick. "Thank you, Kiki." She seemed genuinely pleased, and Kiki was glad she had made the offer. "The door to the basement is over there." She pointed to a door at the other end of the kitchen. "I'll go get my raincoat, and then I'm ready, Lorne. It's pretty blustery out there." She rummaged in a cupboard, pulled out a flashlight, tested it, and set it on the counter. "Just in case the power goes out," she said to Kiki as she left the room.

Kiki had forgotten all about the impending storm. It was so warm and friendly in the Kendricks' house. Kiki didn't really know how to describe the way she felt. *Safe* was the best way to put it.

"Be with you in a minute, hon," Mr. Kendrick said. He was looking at the key and stroking his chin again. "Where did you say you found this?" he asked Kiki.

"Well, actually Pumpkin found it," she said. "It was under one of your rosebushes."

Mr. Kendrick picked the key up from the counter and walked to the back door. He opened it and slipped the key into the outside lock. "It's one of ours, all right," he said, turning it. "But I don't understand how it got out there. We had the locks changed when we moved in. One key fits all the doors. Well, almost all." He pointed to the basement door. "That's the only one in the place with an old-fashioned lock built into the knob. But that door's not strategic to security. Only a starving dwarf could get in through the basement windows."

Kiki smiled and nodded, remembering the narrow window by the rosebush.

"I had three keys made—one for Susan and one for me and a spare. And the spare should be right inside this cupboard." He opened the door to reveal neat stacks of plates and bowls, and a line of cups hanging from hooks. Off to one side was another hook, screwed into the wood. The hook was empty. "That's where it should have been," he said, hanging the key on the hook. "I can't figure how it got outside."

Kiki shrugged. "Maybe Mrs. Kendrick was pruning roses or working in the yard or something, and dropped it."

"I doubt it. She hates yardwork. Honey!" he yelled. "Were you working in the front yard today?"

"Me? I don't do yardwork, remember?" Mrs. Kendrick called back, laughing. "As a matter of fact, this afternoon I hired a man to do the yard. He happened to come by just as I was thinking I'd have to find someone. He's coming next week. He wanted to start right away, but I told him we were going out tonight and I wouldn't have time to show him what I wanted done. Come on, Lorne! We're going to be late!"

Kiki walked to the entry hall to see them out.

"I showed you the intercom system, didn't I?" Mrs. Kendrick asked. "It's programmed to pick

14

up sounds from Jeffrey's room. When he's in there, you can hear him from any room in the house."

Kiki nodded.

"The panel is over the kitchen counter. The buttons are labeled, and you can change it to activate the mike in any room."

"I won't need to change it," Kiki said.

"Jeffrey didn't nap today, so he'll probably get sleepy soon. But he can play with Pumpkin for a while."

"Okay," said Kiki. She could tell Mrs. Kendrick was nervous about leaving.

"Come on, Susan," Mr. Kendrick teased. "We're going to be late. Kiki is very responsible. If she weren't, you wouldn't have hired her."

Mrs. Kendrick smiled. "I know. I sound like a worried mother. But there is one last thing." She looked apologetically at Kiki. "Don't let Pumpkin into Jeffrey's room. I'm sure it's an old wives' tale, but I've heard stories about cats curling up with children and smothering them."

"Susan! That cat doesn't stay still long enough to smother anybody," said Mr. Kendrick, watching appreciatively as Jeffrey chased Pumpkin around the living room. "I predict that they'll both self-destruct in about ten minutes. Maybe less. Bye, Kiki. We'll see you a little after ten."

15

Kiki closed the door firmly behind them and locked it. She listened as the car pulled out of the garage and headed down the street. Her two charges had moved their zone of action to the hallway and were romping down its length, sliding into the kitchen, circling the room, and charging back down the hall to the entryway. There was nothing in the hall to impede their action, and since they were, for the moment, amusing each other, Kiki dodged the hurtling, giggling, screeching bodies and went down to the basement to unload the dryer. "Be right up," she called.

She had just pulled out the last of the towels and dumped them in the basket when she heard a door slam. She froze. Had it been the door to the basement? The light from the kitchen that had illuminated the staircase had disappeared. She ran up the stairs and turned the knob. It wouldn't turn. She pushed. The door wouldn't open. Pumpkin and Jeffrey must have bumped into the door and closed it. She was locked in the basement!

On the other side of the door she could hear the two of them as they careened from kitchen to hallway, playing their silly game. Only now it was more than a game. It was potential disaster. Her crazy cat and the child she was being paid to look after were charging through this big house, unattended. And they could change the racetrack location anytime. She envisioned living room lamps being knocked over (could a broken lamp start a fire?), bathrooms being ransacked (could Jeffrey fall into the tub and hit his head?), bookcases toppling—Kiki's imagination conjured up every possible horror while she struggled to force the locked door open.

But the horror she was yet to face did not even occur to her.

Chapter Two

Kiki sat at the top of the steep staircase that led to the main floor of the house and assessed her situation. In the kitchen, which was just inches from where she was sitting, she could hear Jeffrey and Pumpkin circling the room.

"Jeffrey!" she called. "Jeffrey, can you hear me?" Kiki pounded on the door, but with no results. How much longer would they keep it up, she wondered, before the little boy got tired or cranky or had to go to the bathroom? What would happen when Pumpkin had had enough and simply collapsed in a warm corner somewhere for a catnap, as he did frequently? The sounds became faint. They must be in the hall or the entryway. She stood up and turned around. Maybe she could force the door open. She braced herself on the top step and threw her weight against the door. The thud was impressive, but the door didn't budge. Kiki rubbed her hip and wished silently that she had more meat on her lanky frame.

There had to be a way to get back into the house! Then Kiki had an inspiration. Maybe the Kendricks kept their tools in the basement. She ran down the stairs and canvassed the area. There was a workbench along one wall, with a shop light hanging over it. Kiki pushed the button on the hanging fixture and fluorescent light flooded the area, throwing misshapen shadows on the wall. The top of the bench was bare, but a drawer yielded a hammer and screwdriver. Maybe she could remove the doorknob! That was where the lock was. Mr. Kendrick had said so!

Grasping the tools tightly in one hand, she ran back up the stairs and slid the screwdriver under the circular brass plate surrounding the knob. Her mother had done that the year before, when she had repainted a bedroom door. Tapping the screwdriver gently with the hammer, she wedged it under the metal until the disc swung free, but the knob remained firmly in place. Kiki squinted at the knob. There were two small screws, one on either side. If she could remove them, maybe the knob would come off. The temporary warmth from the dryer had dissipated, and her cold hands had difficulty guiding the blade of the screwdriver into the slot on the head of the screws. *Slow down. Take it easy,* she said to herself. The flat-bladed screwdriver was not made to fit the Phillips-head screws, and she had to angle the point into the grooves to get it to grip. Slowly, slowly she worked, until finally—success! One of the screws dropped to the stair. She could wiggle the knob! The other screw proved more difficult, and she willed herself to concentrate, despite the nagging knowledge that the noises in the kitchen had stopped. Where were the two of them now? Bedroom? Den? Living room?

The top of the stairs was only dimly lit. She could barely see what she was doing. She gave the screwdriver one final turn and the screw came free. But the feeling of success was fleeting, as the brass knob came off in her hand, leaving the inside kitchen knob in place and the lock mechanism still securely fastened. "Darn," said Kiki out loud, feeling frustrated and cold.

She went back to the workbench to find something, anything, that would help her gain access to the kitchen. It was obvious that neither Mr. nor Mrs. Kendrick were particularly handy around the house, since there were no tools to speak of. *Why couldn't I be sitting for a plumber?* she said to herself. *Or a carpenter? Or better yet, a locksmith?* Kiki put the hammer and screwdriver back in the drawer. As she reached up to turn off the shop light, she noticed a speaker built into the wall above the bench. The intercom! The Kendricks had had the intercom system installed in the basement, too!

She turned up the volume and listened. She knew the mike was turned on in Jeffrey's room. If Jeffrey and Pumpkin were in there, she'd pick up something. At first all she heard was a rustling noise, which she assumed was the sound of the wind rushing outside as it carried the storm closer. She stood on tiptoe and leaned over the bench, putting her ear up against the speaker. Or *was* that the wind? No! She realized that she heard that sound every night, when Pumpkin jumped into bed beside her and curled up on the extra pillow, right next to her ear! That was the familiar sound of a contented, tired, sleeping cat. Kiki smiled ruefully. So much for keeping the cat out of Jeffrey's room! But where was Jeffrey? She listened again. There was another sound: the soft, rhythmic breathing of a child. There were a few quick snorts, and then deep breathing again. They'd both conked out!

Now, if they'll both just stay asleep until I get out of here, she thought. She reached up again and turned off the shop light. She'd have to search for a different way out.

Kiki walked the perimeter of the basement. There were three small windows, including the

22

one by the rosebush. But even if she did manage to squeeze through one of them, how would she get back inside the house? Oh, how she wished she still had that key in her pocket! She closed her eyes and saw Mr. Kendrick deliberately placing it back on the hook in the cupboard. Big help it was there!

She had to get out of this basement! As long as things were under control upstairs, she had a little time. She went back to the speaker to reassure herself. Both the cat and the baby were still making sleeping noises.

She checked out the windows again. At basement-ceiling level, they were latched from inside, and opened out when she undid the latch and pushed. Two were impossible—one butted up against a tree trunk, and the other was wired shut. That left the one by the rosebush. She didn't look forward to crawling under the thorns again, and there was no guarantee that she could get back inside the house, but she had to try it. Maybe the Kendricks had left a window open.

"Okay, Kiki," she said to herself, heading toward the third window. "You are about to become, in Mr. Kendrick's words, a starving dwarf."

The latch was stiff and she struggled to push the handle up to release it. The single bare bulb over the washer and dryer was halfway across the large room, and the far edge of the room was in shadow.

This window probably hasn't been opened for years! Kiki thought.

She drew in her breath and gave the latch one fierce push. It swung up. "That's half the battle," she said under her breath. Kiki shoved on the window frame. It opened an inch and then stuck. Then she thought of the hammer. She was sure she could open it with that. And she needed something to stand on so she could reach the window better. Kiki hurried back to the workbench and retrieved the hammer, took a quick listen at the speaker to make sure everything was okay, and dragged a wooden box over to the window. She was standing on the box, just ready to force the window open with the hammer, when the lights of a vehicle swept the driveway in front of the house and past the little basement window.

Kiki stayed very still on the box. She assumed the Kendricks must have forgotten something. The lights went out and the noisy engine stopped. A door slammed, and another. *The minute they get inside they'll realize what happened,* Kiki thought. She climbed off the box, ran up the stairs, and pounded on the door to the kitchen. But there was no response.

Where are the Kendricks? The question had barely taken shape in her mind when a beam of light flashed through the basement window. Kiki crouched on the stairs, motionless. Someone was in the flower bed by the rosebush, right at the spot where Pumpkin had found the key!

Kiki's heart was pounding and an inexplicable feeling of fear swept over her. Whoever was out there, it was not the Kendricks. She crept to the bottom of the stairs and back over to the box by the window. A leg appeared, and then another. They belonged to a man wearing cowboy boots and jeans. She shifted her head for a better look.

A hand dropped down in front of her nose, and she almost lost her balance on the box. The fragile pane of glass between the hand and her face gave little protection, but the intruder seemed too intent on looking for something even to notice the slightly opened window or the frightened girl crouching on the other side.

"Get that light over here, Shorty!" a gruff voice said. "I can't find it!"

The beam from a flashlight zeroed in on the ground under the rosebush and, in its light, Kiki could see that a tarp had been thrown over the bush as protection against the thorns. The hand stirred the dirt in the bed.

"It's not here," the man said.

"Get out of there, Leo, and let me look," said

another voice in a throaty whisper. "I know where I put it!" The man had a clipped accent that sounded British. The cowboy boots gave way to a much larger pair of canvas hightops. They were an odd color. Kiki peered through the window. They were purple!

The man squatted down in the flower bed, and Kiki noticed that he seemed very tall and broad-shouldered. She wondered briefly about his nickname, Shorty. "I put it right here!" he said in a puzzled tone.

You sure did, thought Kiki. *I know what you're looking for. The key. And you can look until doomsday, but you won't find it, because Pumpkin found it first!*

"Look at this!" Shorty continued. "This bed has been scratched up. And this window wasn't open before."

Kiki held her breath and pressed herself up against the basement wall.

"So Kendrick wanted to air out his basement," said the other man. "What's the big deal?"

"I don't like it, Leo. Who could have found it? This plan was foolproof. I've never done anything so easy. His wife bought my gardener story hook, line, and sinker. Even invited me in for a spot of tea while she explained what she wanted done. That's when I saw the key hanging

26

right there in the cupboard. She was getting out the cups, and the doorbell rang, so I just took it while she went to the door."

"It would have been foolproof if you'd kept the key, you lamebrain. Putting it in the flower bed was stupid."

"Sure! With my record, that's all I'd need. Getting picked up with a key to the D.A.'s house in my pocket."

"You don't even know that it was a key to the house!"

"No, but there was a good chance it was. And getting in with a key is a fair shake better than breaking and entering!"

"Well, we're back to breaking and entering," said the man named Leo. "And we'd better move, or they'll be home and we'll have to deal with more than just a babysitter. The car pulled out half an hour ago, and they didn't have the kid with them!"

"I told you, she called the sitter while I was having tea in the garden. She told her to come at seven instead of six-thirty."

That's the call Mom took, Kiki thought.

The voices grew fainter as the men moved from the flower bed. "This may be our last chance to get our hands on that . . ."

Kiki's heartbeat pounded in her ears. They

were going to break into the house. And Pumpkin and Jeffrey were in there, alone!

She stayed very still for a few moments, trying to calm herself. Her mind was racing a mile a minute. Could this be the pair that had burglarized the other neighborhood homes? Something intuitive told her no. While they had showed up right after the Kendricks had left, which was what had happened in the other burglaries, one of them had been here before. They weren't ordinary burglars. They were after something specific. She wished she could have heard what it was they were looking for. What did the Kendricks have that was so valuable? Whatever it was, she had to stop them!

With strength she didn't know she possessed, Kiki forced the window open and, twisting her body like a corkscrew, worked her way out through the cramped space until she could wrap her arms around the rosebush. Ignoring the thorns tearing through her sweatshirt, she yanked first her torso, then her legs, out through the sash, and crawled to the edge of the flower bed. One thing she knew for certain: now she wouldn't have to worry about finding a window open. Wherever the men entered, she would, too.

Staying close to the house so she wouldn't be seen, Kiki started searching for where the men

28

had gotten into the house. As she crept along she tried to program her mind to think like a burglar. If she weren't so scared, she might have laughed. Pretending to be a burglar in the new D.A.'s house! Well, someone, or two someones, were doing more than pretending. *Let's see . . .* said Kiki to herself. The front of the house was not a good entry point. It was too exposed to anyone in the street, and besides, the plate-glass windows were large. Breaking one of them would surely alert anyone in the house. She smiled grimly. *But there's no one in the house,* she thought, *except a two-year-old and a cat.* Both still sleeping, she hoped.

She tiptoed down by the garage, stopping long enough to take note of the truck in the driveway. A Ford. Old. No license plate front or back. Left headlight damaged. Dark color, navy blue or black. Kiki gave silent thanks to Andrew Carlisle, her friend and editor at the school paper. "A story is worthless without the details," he had told her once. "You always have to observe what's going on around you." She wished there were a street light closer so she could see more.

There were no windows on the garage side to give access to the house, so she circled around to the backyard. This was the route they had taken, all right. The men had left the gate open.

29

Cautiously she peeked around the corner and squinted into the darkness to see where they had gone. They weren't in sight.

Storm clouds had completely covered the sky by this time, and the wind had not slackened. Something hit her face. Kiki jumped. A raindrop. Another fell, and another. Her hands were clammy and all her senses were strained to their maximum as she crept across the patio, listening and watching for the burglars. It was raining hard now, a cold rain driven by the wind into a stinging spray.

The only light visible came from the kitchen window. A twig snapped. Kiki stopped, every nerve on alert. Had she made the noise or had they? Or was it the wind? She crept around the corner to the west side of the house. There were no apparent lights, and Kiki wished she had the flashlight that Mrs. Kendrick had set out in case of a power failure. She looked up at a dark window and mentally reviewed the floor plan. This would be Mr. Kendrick's home office—a room lined with law books and dominated by a huge mahogany desk with a compatibly large leather swivel chair, and an old console TV in one corner. Mrs. Kendrick had shown her the room the week before, laughingly explaining away the clutter with a wave of her hand. "He does as much work here as he does downtown," she had said.

Boxes of papers—cases Mr. Kendrick had tried in court, Kiki supposed—lined the back wall, and a computer sat on a stand beside the desk. She remembered that there was a phone on the desk in that room. If she could get inside, she could use that phone to call for help. The kitchen was out, since the ceiling lights were so bright that she'd never get to the kitchen phone without being seen. She turned the corner and moved along the west side of the house.

At the last window on that side, the tarp that the men had used to cover the rosebush was lying on the ground in a heap. She looked up. The window was open. This would be the master bedroom, Kiki thought as she cautiously stood on tiptoe to peer in. If they were after Mrs. Kendrick's jewelry, this would be the room they'd want. Kiki had noticed that Mrs. Kendrick was wearing an elegant diamond brooch that night, and that her rings looked very expensive.

But there didn't appear to be anyone in the bedroom. Kiki swallowed. What if the men weren't burglars? What if they were kidnappers and were after Jeffrey? She pushed the thought aside. She had to get back in the house. There might not be any time to lose!

31

Kiki took a deep breath and, putting her hands flat on the outside sill, boosted herself up. With one final push she toppled headfirst into the room. The carpeted floor muffled the sound of her fall, and she lay there for a moment, listening. There was not a sound but the wind.

Where were they?

Kiki tiptoed to the doorway and looked down the hall. The faint glow of a flashlight was coming from Mr. Kendrick's office. What were they doing in there? She held her breath and listened. They were arguing about something, and every few seconds she heard a drawer slam. She decided they must be going through the desk, drawer by drawer.

"Give me some light over here! I can't see a thing!"

"It isn't going to be in the desk! Check the TV, and those boxes."

Grotesque shadows leaped out through the doorway as the men moved through the room with the flashlight.

"Just papers, that's all. Just papers."

The intercom speaker by the bed crackled, and the unmistakable cry of a child followed. Jeffrey! Jeffrey was awake! If she could hear him, so could the men. She had to get to a phone to call for help. There was a phone on the nightstand. Kiki ran to it and, with shaking hands, lifted the receiver. But there was no light on the dial, and no dial tone. Nothing. The line was dead. Raw fear washed over her. The storm? Or had the men cut the wires outside the house?

Abandoning caution, she ran back to the door just in time to hear Leo say, "Shorty, let's take the kid. Maybe I can barter for it." They were coming down the hall toward her, heading for the front of the house. She'd have to go right by them to get to Jeffrey's room.

"Where do you think the sitter is?" asked Shorty. "We better find her first. Let's check the living room. Kendrick didn't leave the kid here alone. I tell you, I heard the wife call the sitter!"

The sentence was barely out of his mouth when a wild yowl erupted from the front of the house. It was Pumpkin!

Yeeeoooww!

"Ooowww!"

It was hard to separate the human cries from the animal's outraged screeches.

"Ow! Bloody little turd bit my ankle! Get him! There he is!"

"What's he got in his mouth? Ouch! That hurts!"

Something crashed as the men careened around in the dark, trying to avoid an angry Pumpkin.

Yeeeoooww!

"Get this dratted cat off me! Hit him! Hit him with the flashlight!"

"I'm trying! Ow! The little monster bit my hand!"

Way to go, Pumpkin! Kiki thought. *Great timing. Create a diversion.*

Pumpkin could be a formidable foe if he took a dislike to someone. The paper carrier had once told Kiki that he'd rather take his chances with a crocodile than be chased by her cat.

"Ouch!"

Crash!

This was her chance! Kiki raced to the entry hall and turned toward the open doorway of Jeffrey's room.

"There she is!" one of the men yelled.

The beam of the flashlight flared on her momentarily as he ran toward her and lunged at the door. Kiki was too fast for him but, luckily, not for Pumpkin. He catapulted into the room just as she slammed the door in the man's face and turned the lock. Her breath was coming in short gasps and her knees felt rubbery. She wanted to sit down, but she couldn't let down her guard now. What if they tried to break the door down? She glanced quickly around the room. There was a three-drawer chest up against one wall. She shoved it over in front of the door, tipped it on its side with a loud crash, and piled a chair and a small table on top. Pumpkin leaped to the summit of the furniture mountain and snarled.

The men were having a conference in loud whispers outside the door.

"Kidnapping's heavy-duty, Leo. You're talking a life sentence if we get caught! Give me a fifty-fifty split and I might consider it."

Pumpkin snarled again.

"No way. Okay, forget taking the kid. Let's just take a look in the kid's room and get out of here before Kendrick gets back. It could be in there."

Another snarl, louder.

"In a kid's room? Kendrick's not going to put it in his kid's room!"

"He might. Every kid's got a tube in their room these days."

"This kid's just a baby! Besides, the sitter's got that wildcat in there with her."

"Maybe you're right. Better in there with her than out here with us!"

Kiki looked nervously at the lightweight door that stood between her and the intruders and snatched up a heavy wooden truck from the toy box, ready to defend herself and Jeffrey if she had to. They'd probably have no trouble forcing the lock. She stared in silence as the doorknob turned and the door rattled, but the flimsy lock held.

With a wild scream, Pumpkin attacked the door.

"Come on, it's not going to be in there. I tell you, if it's here, it's in that other room. And the sitter's not going anywhere until we're out of here!" Shorty raised his voice so Kiki could hear him clearly. "And you're not making any phone calls, are you, honey? We made sure of that!" A nasty laugh punctuated his speech.

"I've already called the police," Kiki yelled back. "From the basement while you were out in the flower bed. The police are on the way. You've had it."

There was a hurried consultation outside the door and then silence. When she was sure they'd gone back down the hall, Kiki moved to the bed and sat down beside Jeffrey, who was sitting up and listening with interest, unaware of the potential danger. Kiki nuzzled the top of his head and held onto him tightly. His hair smelled of shampoo, and the warmth of his flannel-clad body up against hers gave her some comfort. She realized then that she was trembling.

What were they after? They had been talking about splitting some money, and then there was something about a tube.

"Kitty!" said Jeffrey, wiggling to get free of her grasp.

Pumpkin responded instantly, jumping up on

the bed and curling up beside them. Kiki held the little boy and stroked the cat for a long time. Finally, she heard the truck's motor turn over . . . and then die. It turned over again. On the third try, the engine roared noisily, and she waited until she heard it fade into the distance before she moved the furniture and unlocked the door.

From off in another part of the house, the chimes of a clock sounded. Kiki turned on the bedside lamp and looked at her watch. It was only eight-thirty, but it felt like midnight.

She was heading for the living room to assess the damage when she heard a key turn in the front door lock.

"Oh, no, what now?" she moaned. She stood motionless in the entry hall, her face drained of color, and stared as the front door opened.

Chapter Three

"Kiki!" said Mr. Kendrick, bursting in through the front door with his wife. "You're white as a sheet! What happened here? We tried to call but the phone was dead!"

"Is Jeffrey all right?" said Mrs. Kendrick breathlessly.

Kiki let out her breath with relief. Slowly, the color came back to her face. "Jeffrey's okay," she said. "He didn't even know anything happened. They didn't see him."

As if to reinforce her words, Jeffrey sauntered down the hall dragging the wooden truck that Kiki had been ready to use as a weapon. Close behind, batting playfully at the truck with his paw, was a very tame, very domesticated Pumpkin.

Mrs. Kendrick rushed over to the little boy and hugged him to her. "My baby!" she said. "We were so worried!"

"Who was here, Kiki? What are you talking about?" Mr. Kendrick asked.

"Two burglars," Kiki replied. "We were just robbed."

"Oh, no!" said Mrs. Kendrick. She picked up Jeffrey and took Kiki by the arm. "Oh, Kiki! How horrible! Are you all right? Come over here and sit down." She led Kiki into the living room and sat down beside her on the couch.

Kiki looked at a broken lamp on the living-room floor. "That must have been the crash I heard when Pumpkin attacked them," she mused.

Mr. Kendrick took Jeffrey from his wife's arms and planted a kiss on his head. "Kiss your mom now, and then it's back to bed for you!" Mr. Kendrick started down the hall. "I'll be right back," he said over his shoulder.

"Let's go to the kitchen," Mrs. Kendrick said. "I'll fix you a hot drink." Kiki followed her and sat on one of the stools at the counter. She was suddenly very tired.

"How about some hot chocolate?" said Mrs. Kendrick, nervously moving from cupboard to sink to refrigerator. "You look wiped out."

"I *am* wiped out," Kiki started to say. But before she had finished the sentence, Pumpkin appeared from nowhere and jumped up on the counter.

40

"Hello!" said Mrs. Kendrick. She tried to keep her tone light, but her voice was still shaking. "I guess I said that magic word, didn't I?" She ruffled the cat's fur. "I understand you were a hero tonight, so I'll make you some, too!"

"Now, Kiki, tell us what happened," said Mr. Kendrick, striding into the kitchen. He gave her an appraising glance. "Your sweatshirt's all torn up. And is that blood?"

Kiki looked down at her shirt. "That's from the rosebush," she explained. She pushed up her sleeves and checked her arms. There were deep scratches on both of them.

"Oh, dear," said Mrs. Kendrick. "Let me get something for that!" She put a mug of steaming hot chocolate in front of Kiki and a saucer before Pumpkin, who purred his appreciation.

Kiki shook her head. "No, I'm okay. Really. They're just scratches. They don't even hurt." But Mrs. Kendrick was already reaching into a cupboard for some antiseptic.

"Thank goodness we came home, Lorne," she said as she treated Kiki's arms. "You know, Kiki, it was really a fluke. I tried to call you just to see how things were going, but the line was dead. At first I thought it was the storm, but the operator said everyone else in the neighborhood had service, so I got worried."

"What happened, Kiki?" Mr. Kendrick repeated.

"Well, right after you left I went down to the basement for just a minute to get the clothes out of the dryer. Pumpkin and Jeffrey were playing in the kitchen. Somehow they accidentally closed the door, and it locked."

Kiki kept talking until she had told them everything. How she had monitored Jeffrey and Pumpkin on the basement intercom; how she had crawled out the basement window and climbed in the bedroom window; how Pumpkin had attacked the intruders; and finally how she had run down to Jeffrey's room and barricaded the door. "I'm really sorry," she said, looking from one to the other.

"Sorry? You have nothing to apologize for!" said Mrs. Kendrick.

"No, indeed," said Mr. Kendrick. "You did a great job of keeping Jeffrey safe under the worst possible circumstances!"

"Then you're not angry because I got locked in the basement?"

Mr. Kendrick shook his head. "No. That was a providential accident. That was the best place you could have been, because it gave you an element of surprise over the burglars. You handled yourself very well. Although next time, you *might* consider running to the neighbors to call the police!" he teased. "Come and show me where the men were. I can't find anything missing."

"Speaking of the police," said Mrs. Kendrick, "I'm going to call them now."

Kiki led the new D.A. from room to room. It didn't appear as if anything had been taken from Mrs. Kendrick's jewel box, and the stereo, TV, VCR, and compact disc player were in place. When they got to Mr. Kendrick's office, he looked around the room quickly. "There's nothing here that they'd want," he said. "It's all legal stuff. No resale value. Except for the computer, and the only part of it that's missing is the mouse. I found it in the living room." He pulled the computer mouse from his pocket. "They ripped it out and then didn't take it."

"May I see it?" Kiki asked.

Mr. Kendrick handed over the mouse and a big grin spread across Kiki's face as she examined it.

"I don't think the burglars ripped it out," she said. "Look at those teeth marks on the cord."

"Pumpkin?" he asked.

Kiki nodded. "I think he grabbed the cord in his mouth and swung it so the mouse would hit at ankle level."

Right on cue, Pumpkin appeared and jumped at Kiki, grabbing the computer mouse from her hand. Clamping his teeth on the stretchable coiled cord, he swung himself around in circles at dizzying speed.

Kiki and Mr. Kendrick backed away as the mouse flew in a circle, cracking against everything within its circumference.

"Very clever, Pumpkin!" Kiki said, grabbing the cat's improvised weapon in flight. "Thanks for the demonstration!"

Mr. Kendrick looked puzzled. "I can't figure it. Why would they break in and not take anything?"

"It sounded like they were after something specific," Kiki said. "They kept coming back to this room. And they talked about a tube—the TV, I guess. The one named Shorty was the man Mrs. Kendrick interviewed for the gardener's job. He's the one who stole the key."

"So *that* explains it!" said Mr. Kendrick. "Leave it to the British to charm a lady," he added with a wry grin. "But what could they have been looking for?. . ."

They finished the tour and went back to the kitchen just as Mrs. Kendrick came in from the garage. "I called the police on the car phone," she said. "They're sending someone over. They'll want a statement from you, Kiki. Are you up to that?"

Kiki nodded. "I'm okay," she said.

They waited almost an hour before the officers arrived, and when they did, one of them had Kiki repeat the entire story again while he took notes. Then he started asking her questions.

"Can you tell me what they looked like?"

"Not really," Kiki replied. "I only saw their feet clearly. One had on purple hightop sneakers and the other one was wearing cowboy boots. When I saw them later, inside the house, it was dark. I couldn't tell what their faces looked like. I think they were wearing stockings over their heads, because their hair was flattened down."

"Were they large, like Mr. Kendrick?"

"The one called Leo was shorter and thinner than Mr. Kendrick. The other one, Shorty, was big. He had a British accent. Mrs. Kendrick could describe him for you. She saw him this afternoon."

"I've already talked to Mrs. Kendrick," he said curtly. "I'm questioning you right now. Color of hair?"

"I don't know. It was dark. I really only saw their feet."

The officer looked up at her. "The department should start a foot file to go with the mug shots they keep," he muttered. "Would you be able to identify them from photographs?"

Kiki shook her head. "Can't you look for fingerprints or footprints or something like that?" she asked.

"The other officer is doing that now, but often the results are inconclusive. We like to get information from an eyewitness first. Now, let me check what I have. You were here alone with the little boy, right?"

Kiki nodded. "Except my cat was here, too." Pumpkin stretched lazily on the carpet, pointing with his hind legs.

"Yes," said the officer. "But I don't think your cat could be a reliable witness." Pumpkin got up. His tail shot into the air, exhibiting his disapproval. The police officer ignored him.

"You saw their vehicle?" he asked.

"Yes," Kiki said. "It was an old Ford truck, either black or navy blue."

"Which?" asked the policeman.

"I couldn't tell. It was too dark."

The officer frowned. "How old is *old*?" he asked. "Two years? Five years? Ten years?"

Kiki suddenly had the feeling that she was being interrogated like a criminal rather than a witness, and she resented it.

"At least ten years old," she snapped. "And in bad shape. There was a big scrape on the driver's side, like he'd sideswiped something, and the left headlight was smashed."

The officer shifted position. "License number?" he asked, raising one eyebrow ever so slightly.

"It didn't have plates, front or back."

He closed his notebook and looked at her. "Any other observations?"

Kiki concentrated, trying to remember. "Just one thing," she said. "There was something dangling from the rearview mirror. One of those car ornaments. It looked like a fuzzy monkey."

He opened his notebook again and wrote something down. Then he yawned, and Kiki realized that he was probably as tired as she was. She regretted being snappish.

"I'm sorry I can't tell you more about them," she said.

"That's all right," said the police officer. "Better that you tell the truth than make up something. And under the circumstances," he added, "you remembered quite a bit." He smiled. "Here," he said, handing Kiki a slip of paper with a name and number on it. "If you remember anything else tomorrow, call me."

"Some more coffee?" Mrs. Kendrick asked him.

"No, thanks. Officer Rawlins should be winding it up soon. I'll go out and wait for her." He was gathering his things when the back door opened and Mr. Kendrick and the other police officer came in. She was a heavyset black

47

woman. She smiled at Kiki, who by now had Pumpkin curled up in her lap.

"This must be our attack cat!" she said, scratching Pumpkin behind the ears. "And you must be Miss Collier."

Kiki nodded. "Did you find anything out there?"

"There are a couple of footprints by the rose-bush," she said, "but the fingerprints on the sill where they entered are smudged."

"That's because I slid in over them," Kiki said, frowning. "Big help, wiping out evidence."

"You did what you had to do," Officer Rawlins said.

"What about the office? Or the living room?"

Mr. Kendrick grinned. "The only concrete clues we found in there were some tufts of orange cat fur, and we know where *they* came from!"

Kiki nodded. "Did you get any prints off Jeffrey's doorknob? I know they touched that. I stood inside and watched it turn."

"I dusted it. There wasn't much there."

The police left, and Kiki put Pumpkin in her backpack.

"Kiki, you're welcome to spend the night, or at least stay here until your mother gets home," Mrs. Kendrick said, "if you're nervous about being home alone."

"Thanks. I'm okay now, I think."

"Well, you're not walking. I'm driving you home," Mr. Kendrick said in a tone that left no room for argument. Kiki followed him to the garage.

"Didn't they take anything at all, then?" she asked.

"A three-strand pearl necklace of Susan's is missing from the bedroom," Mr. Kendrick said. "But they left an antique opal ring that was sitting out on the dressing table."

"Were the pearls valuable?"

"No. Nineteen-ninety-five from the local department store where we used to live. I can't figure out what they were after. They had a truck. They could have taken the TV, or the VCR, or my computer, or the microwave. They all have resale value. That's the puzzler."

Kiki leaned back against the luxuriously padded car seat. "They were after something in your office," she said. "That's where they spent most of their time."

"Beats me," said Mr. Kendrick. "Maybe they were looking for a wall safe. Some homes have them." He pulled into the Colliers' driveway and handed Kiki a twenty-dollar bill.

"Oh, this is way too much!" she protested.

"You earned it. I'm paying for your intelligence, ingenuity, and gumption!"

Meeeooow! Pumpkin poked his head out of the backpack.

"Yours, too, Pumpkin!" said Mr. Kendrick, scratching behind the cat's ears. "I feel terrible that this happened, Kiki. We'd like you to come back and sit for Jeffrey again, if you're not spooked by the idea."

Kiki shook her head, but before she could say anything, Mr. Kendrick continued, "I'll have bolts put on the windows tomorrow and I'm going to change the door locks again, just in case they copied the key."

"Okay," said Kiki, getting out of the car. "Thanks." She attempted a smile. "Some welcome to the neighborhood, huh?"

Mr. Kendrick arched his eyebrows. "Well," he said, "on the bright side, we *have* found a brave babysitter who comes complete with a four-legged burglar alarm."

Kiki laughed, feeling slightly embarrassed, and went inside.

Once in the house, Kiki let Pumpkin out of her backpack, then looked at her watch. It was almost midnight. She debated leaving a note for her mother. After Kiki's dad had been killed, her mother went back to full-time work at the hospital. Since on some days Kiki and Dr. Collier saw each other only briefly at breakfast or dinner, they had agreed to leave notes for each other under the big daisy magnet on the refrigerator. Actually, the notes had been Dr. Collier's idea. At first Kiki had thought they were a pain, but eventually she had gotten into the habit and, on some occasions, even enjoyed penning notes to her mother.

But this wasn't one of those occasions. It was too long a story to put in a note, and she was too tired to wait up and tell it all again. Furthermore, if she left a note that said something like, *Hi, Mom, the Kendricks' house was robbed tonight while I was babysitting*, her mother would have a conniption fit. *Better to wait till morning and tell her in person*, Kiki thought sleepily.

Chapter Four

Kiki's alarm rang for a long time the next morning before she even heard it, and when she did, she turned it off and went back to sleep until her mother called her. She dressed slowly, her head groggy from a troubled sleep filled with nightmares. When she got downstairs for breakfast, Dr. Collier was still in her bathrobe, sitting at the kitchen table with a cup of coffee and the morning newspaper.

"Hi, sweets!" she said, looking up. "No note! How did it go at the Kendricks'?"

Kiki settled herself in a chair across from her mother.

"And where did you get those scratches?" said Dr. Collier, looking at her more critically.

"You wouldn't believe it," Kiki said, and told her what had happened.

"Oh, Kiki, how horrible!" Dr. Collier's face paled, and she reached over and took Kiki's hand. "I'm so grateful you're all right! I would have been scared stiff!"

"I guess I was, but I didn't have time to think about it."

"Your dad would have hit the roof! His little girl fending off burglars and kidnappers!" She gave a wry laugh, then looked around the kitchen. "Where's Pumpkin? I'm going to learn to appreciate that cat yet!"

"Upstairs sleeping," Kiki replied, a small lump coming into her throat at the mention of her dad. "He doesn't have first-period math." She slapped the side of her head lightly with her hand. "Yikes! I didn't get my homework done. Old Tanning will be on my case for sure!"

"Just explain what happened. Surely he'll make an allowance for that."

"No excuse short of World War Three would satisfy him. Are you working today?"

Her mother nodded. "I'm at the satellite clinic in Cloverdon from ten till five. I should be home by six. It's only thirty-five miles." She paused, then added, "Sweetheart, be careful."

"Not to worry, Mom. I don't think *those* burglars will be back, not after the way Pumpkin took care of them. I'm sure they're suffering a few scratches themselves today. And I *don't* mean from the rosebushes!" She kissed her mother's cheek. "See you later! I'll fix us some

54

tacos for dinner. I think I've figured out how to do it without cremating the shells." Kiki grabbed her backpack from the front hall and slammed the door behind her.

Andrew was locking his bike when Kiki skidded to a stop at the racks. "What do we have going today, editor?" she asked as she looped a cable through the frame of her own bike. "Anything newsworthy?"

Andrew was editor of the Pioneer Junior High newspaper, *The Courier*, and Kiki was one of the staff. He was ahead of her by a grade, and older by a year, but they had become good friends in the semester she'd worked on the paper.

"How'd you like to cover the cafeteria?" he teased, brown eyes dancing.

"Give it to Elena!" Kiki replied. "Maybe she'll pick up ptomaine on the way through." She lowered her voice. "We should be so lucky."

"Okay, doc," he said. "What's ptomaine? Enough to shut her up for a couple of hours?"

"Major food poisoning," Kiki said, nodding. "Guaranteed."

Elena Morgan was a ninth grader who worked on the paper. When Cecilia Lambert, faculty adviser to *The Courier*, had appointed Andrew as editor, Elena was not happy. But Andrew had served a two-week summer internship at the local paper and was hoping to make journalism his career. And he had already won a statewide award for writing. Many times Kiki, as the apprentice on the three-person staff, had been the target of Elena's sarcasm, although both Kiki and Andrew admitted that Elena was a good writer and had a nose for news.

Meeeooow!

Kiki stopped walking and turned around. "No!" she said. "He must have sneaked downstairs and out the back door while I was in the kitchen." A twitching nose peeked out from behind a tree in the schoolyard, followed by two pointy ears standing straight up in expectation.

Andrew laughed. "Well, you don't have time to take him back. He can stay up in the *Courier* office with me. I don't have a class first period."

"Well, I do," said Kiki. She snapped her fingers and Pumpkin came running to her. "Tanning, and I didn't get my homework done." Andrew held her backpack while she stowed Pumpkin inside. "Thanks. I had quite a night last night," she continued. The stairs were crowded with students going to class, so Kiki quickly related what had happened. She was so immersed in telling Andrew the sequence of events that she didn't realize until they were at the *Courier* office door that Elena had been close on their heels.

"Sounds like news to me!" Elena said,

smirking at her. "I can see the headline now: *Babysitter Locked in Basement While House Is Robbed.*"

"Get off her back, Elena," said Andrew, pushing the door open. "It's all hearsay to you. You don't have any facts."

Elena slammed her books down on her desk, one of three jammed into the small room. "There are ways to verify the facts," she said, looking at Kiki. "You wouldn't know them, of course."

Eeeoooww!

With a wild leap, Pumpkin rocketed from the backpack and landed on top of Elena's desk, spitting and hissing.

"Do I have to put up with that—that *thing* again?" Elena said, backing away from the angry cat. Pumpkin's long fur resembled a long, orange bristled brush, and his eyes were narrowed to slits. "There's a rule against bringing animals to school!"

Andrew leaned up against the file cabinet. "All the famous writers I've read about had pets," he said. "Hemingway, Jack London, Madeleine L'Engle . . . Besides, we have carte blanche up here, and you know it! If I may quote Lambert, 'My students need to be responsible for what goes on in the newspaper office and what goes out of it. They must learn to take their

57

lumps, because that's what will happen out in the real world of journalism.' End quote."

Meow! Pumpkin jumped down and rubbed against Andrew's leg.

"Well, keep him away from me," Elena said. "I'm allergic to cats."

"Looks like the feeling is mutual," said Andrew as Pumpkin leaped to the windowsill, as far from the black-haired girl as he could get, and hissed. "Smart cat," Andrew whispered, just loudly enough for Kiki to hear.

The bell rang. "I'm outta here!" Kiki said, and with a grateful grin at Andrew and a final pat for Pumpkin, she disappeared into the crowd of students in the hall.

Even after hearing an abbreviated explanation, Mr. Tanning was unforgiving about the math assignment. "Hand it in tomorrow," he said. "Only half credit, of course. And a big fat zero if you don't. Illness is the only acceptable excuse."

Kiki slumped in her chair and tried to concentrate, but thinking about the excitement at the Kendricks' and the fact that she was tired made it impossible for her to keep her mind on the classwork. She was both startled and relieved when the voice of the school secretary came over the speaker, summoning her to the principal's office immediately. She picked up her books and left a roomful of curious students behind. A call with that kind of urgency often meant some grave infraction of the rules.

Kiki had it all figured out before she reached the lower floor: Andrew had been called off somewhere, and Elena had seized the opportunity to rat on Pumpkin. She turned the corner and entered the principal's office. Two kids were sitting on the bench in the secretary's area—disciplinary problems, obviously, since one had a ripped shirt and the other was holding a fistful of wet paper towels up against a bloody nose.

"Go right in, Kiki," the secretary said. "They're waiting for you."

They? Puzzled, Kiki opened the door and entered Principal Mucatti's office. She looked around the room quickly. No Pumpkin. A tall, fair-haired man with a neat mustache was waiting with the principal, and he smiled at her as she came in.

"Kiki," said the principal, "this is Detective Pelley from the police department."

The man opened a leather wallet to show her a badge, and then reached out to shake hands. "Plainclothes detective, Miss Collier," he explained, taking in her quizzical look.

"Is this something about last night?" Kiki asked.

Detective Pelley nodded. "Yes, Mr. Kendrick

asked me to come and get you. He'd like to see you at the courthouse. You don't have to go," he added, "but he'd like to talk to you."

"Sure, I can go," Kiki said, "I guess." She looked at Mr. Mucatti for permission.

"You're excused," the principal said. "Pick up a readmit slip from Mrs. Johnson when you get back."

Detective Pelley shook hands with the principal and then opened the door for Kiki to precede him into the hall. They were almost to the front entrance when Kiki remembered Pumpkin.

"Oh," she said, stopping. "Could I go to the newspaper office first? I forgot something. I'll just be a minute!" And without waiting for him to answer, she ran up the stairs, taking the last ones two at a time. Outside the office door she could hear a typewriter clicking. She frowned. She had hoped that Elena would be gone. Now there'd be an interrogation. She opened the door and almost laughed out loud. Elena had built a wall around her desk with three wastebaskets and the typing table, and the hostile enemy was perched on top of the file cabinet, glaring down at her as she typed.

The cat's stare was broken as Kiki entered, and he jumped down to greet her.

"Come on, Pumpkin," she said. "We're going for a ride." She picked up her backpack from the corner and tucked her math book and then the cat inside.

"It's about time you got that hateful cat out of here," Elena said. Pumpkin reared his head out of the pack and hissed a reply. "He's been a royal pain ever since you left. And of course Andrew had to go off somewhere right after." Elena examined her left hand critically. "He practically bit my finger off when I went to move your backpack."

"He's just protecting his turf," Kiki explained, trying to stifle a grin as she mentally pictured the confrontation. "This backpack is his second home."

"Yes, well, the *Courier* office isn't," Elena snapped. "The next time that creature shows up here, I'm turning you in. There's a fatal disease you can get from cat bites, you know!" she said as Kiki started to leave the room. "And why are you out of class in the middle of the period? Where are you going?" she yelled. But Kiki and Pumpkin were already halfway down the staircase.

Detective Pelley was waiting at the front door.

"Ready?" he asked.

"Ready," Kiki replied. "Thanks for waiting."

"No prob."

She looked at him again as he opened the passenger door of a green Dodge sedan. It was as incognito as he was, she thought, glancing at the detective's brown slacks, sport jacket, and open-necked shirt.

"Nobody would ever guess this was a police car," she said, thinking with satisfaction of Elena, who was probably hanging out the window, watching. "Until you get inside." There was an impressive-looking radio under the dash, and as they pulled away from the curb he picked up a microphone and said something unintelligible.

"That's the way we like it," he replied, putting down the mike. The radio crackled with static and a voice called out some numbers.

Eeoow!

Detective Pelley looked at her sharply and frowned.

"Oh, it's just my cat," Kiki explained quickly, pulling Pumpkin from the backpack. "That's why I went back upstairs."

"Do you always take your cat to school with you?"

Kiki grinned. "*Take* is the wrong word. This cat just shows up. Like, surprise!"

"A cat with a mind of her own," said Detective Pelley. "I like that."

"His own," Kiki corrected.

"Sorry, fellow," said Detective Pelley, scratching Pumpkin's orange fur. "You two look like a matched pair. Same color hair," he laughed. "What's his name?"

"Pumpkin."

"Pumpkin, eh? Well, he's certainly the right color. And practically the right size!"

Pumpkin crawled across the seat, stretched out over Detective Pelley's lap, gave a deep sigh, and closed his eyes.

"Hey, he likes you!" Kiki grinned.

"Smart cat!"

"Actually, he got his name sort of by accident. You see," Kiki continued, "I babysit for this family that has four kids, and for the last couple of years, just before Halloween, I've gone with the kids and their mom to a farm outside of town to help them pick out their pumpkins. Each kid gets to pick one. I'm there sort of as an unarmed guard, to keep the kids from getting lost in the pumpkin patch, because their mother can't watch all four at once when they're wandering around in the field. So she takes two and I take two.

"Well, when we went last year, this cat kept following me through the pumpkin patch. Every time I turned around, he was right behind me."

"So the farmer gave him to you?" Detective Pelley asked.

"No," said Kiki. "It's weirder than that. We

got the kids and the pumpkins into the car and came home—"

"Let me guess. The cat was in the trunk with the pumpkins!"

"No. But two days later, when I got out of school, he was sitting by my bike at the bike rack. So I brought him home, and my mom made me call the farmer to tell him I had his cat. Which I did. But get this—this is the really weird part—the farmer said he didn't have an orange long-haired cat. He had two cats, but they were both gray. And he couldn't even remember seeing the cat the day we were there! He said to keep him, because he didn't need another cat. So I named him Pumpkin, because he came from a pumpkin patch, and because the color was right!"

Pumpkin gave a satisfied sigh, as if he approved of his life story, and repositioned himself more comfortably in Detective Pelley's lap.

"That's quite a beginning," the detective said, glancing down at Pumpkin. He turned the car into the driveway that led to the courthouse's underground garage.

"Do you know if they found the two men?" Kiki asked. "Is that why Mr. Kendrick wants to talk to me?"

"I don't think they did," he replied. "Mrs. Kendrick came down and looked at mug shots, but she didn't recognize the man who came to the house. I'll let Mr. Kendrick tell you about it."

He parked the car in a spot marked Official Vehicles Only, and after Kiki had stuffed Pumpkin into her backpack, they rode the elevator to the main floor of the courthouse. Kiki had never been there before, and Detective Pelley took her arm and steered her into line at the security checkpoint in front of the elevator.

It was similar to airport security, which she had been through, but she was surprised to learn that the courthouse also checked its visitors. Detective Pelley moved off to one side to talk to a uniformed police officer while Kiki was screened. Two other officers were working the line. A man walked through the sensors and a buzzer went off. He backed up, sheepishly took a ring of keys from his pocket, and walked through again.

"Put your tote here," one of the officers said to Kiki, indicating the moving rubber belt. Kiki laid her backpack down, only to snatch it back up again when she remembered Pumpkin. But the cat was one step ahead of her. As soon as he felt the moving belt he rammed his way out, frantically treading in place on the track while the pack went through the X-ray machine. Kiki picked him up and cuddled him.

"Sorry, miss. No animals in the courthouse,"

said the officer, trying to hide her surprise. "Only seeing-eye dogs."

Kiki looked up defensively and was about to protest, but Detective Pelley was already at her side.

"Eyewitness," he said to the security officer. He took Pumpkin from Kiki. "We're on our way to the D.A.'s office." He showed her his badge.

The woman rolled her eyes towards the ceiling. "Now I've heard everything," she muttered.

They got on an elevator marked Employees Only and rode up to the fifth floor.

"Thanks," said Kiki. "How did you know Pumpkin was an eyewitness?"

"Lorne told me the story," said Detective Pelley. Little lines crinkled up at the sides of his eyes as he grinned at Pumpkin. "This is quite a cat!"

"Police officers don't have to go through security?" Kiki asked.

The detective shook his head. "Yes and no. Some do, some don't. It depends on the situation."

"What if someone had a badge, but wasn't really an officer?" she asked.

"Good question. Most of the cops who work the courthouse are known by sight to security. When new ones come on, they make a point of introducing themselves. If there's any question, they go through the line like everyone else. What are you doing? Gathering information for your school newspaper?"

Kiki blushed. He could have been reading her mind. "I thought it would make a good article. You know, what goes on at the courthouse besides paying traffic fines and getting marriage licenses." Kiki had noticed signs on the main floor directing people to counters for both services.

"It would," Detective Pelley agreed. "A lot of interesting people, some dangerous, pass through this place every day. Here we are." The elevator stopped and the doors opened.

They walked down the hall to a door marked District Attorney. Detective Pelley opened the door and motioned for Kiki to enter. Mr. Kendrick was talking to a woman seated at a desk.

"Hi, Kiki," he said, coming over to greet her. He grinned at Detective Pelley, who was still carrying the cat. "Well, George, I see you've made friends with our famous cat. Come on in." He led the way into an inner office and motioned for them to sit down. *It looks similar to his office at home*, Kiki thought. Except the boxes of papers looked even messier here. She frowned. There was a band of yellow plastic tape circling the room, dividing the desk area from the boxes.

"Excuse my mess," Mr. Kendrick said, following Kiki's gaze. "We think that the men who broke into the house last night also found a way to get in here."

Of course! Kiki thought. *The yellow tape is separating the crime scene from the rest of the room.*

"We think it happened sometime between two and five this morning," Mr. Kendrick continued. "The custodians went off shift at two, and there was only one person on security during the night. We think it was the same pair, but we don't know how they got in. They may have had help on the inside. There was no sign of forced entry, except to the office door."

Kiki turned and looked. The glass in the inner office door had masking tape in a criss-cross pattern across it, holding it in. One bottom corner piece had been completely broken out.

"There are a couple of reasons why I asked Detective Pelley to bring you down here," Mr. Kendrick said. "I need your help." He looked very authoritative behind the big desk—not much like the man who had carted Jeffrey off to bed and fed Pumpkin chocolate cupcakes the night before. "You're our only link to these men, because you saw them, however fleetingly. Susan couldn't identify the man who came to the house. I thought you might give it a try. Maybe the other one will be in here." He pushed some large books toward her. "Would you take a look through these mug shots and see if anyone looks familiar?"

"Sure," said Kiki, opening the cover. She spent a long time going through the photographs, but no one seemed to resemble the burglars. "I'm sorry," she said. "It was too dark to see. And I think they had stockings over their faces."

"That's all right," said Mr. Kendrick. "Oh, by the way, do you remember seeing my briefcase at the house last night?"

"Yes! It was in the entry hall. I put my pack down beside it when I came in—and then I picked it up again," she said with a grin, "because Pumpkin was in it, and I took it to the kitchen."

"That's what I thought," said Mr. Kendrick. "So I didn't leave it on the commuter flight yesterday afternoon."

"Is it missing?"

He nodded. "I went to get it when I left the house this morning, and I couldn't find it."

"Did it have something in it they'd want to steal?"

"Legal briefs. I have copies of everything that was in it."

"I don't get it," said Kiki. "If they were after your papers, why did they take the pearls, then?"

"Probably to make it look like an ordinary burglary. Kiki, did the men see you at all, even for just a second?"

Kiki nodded. "They saw me when I ran down the hall to Jeffrey's room. But it was dark. They saw a lot more of Pumpkin than they did of me!"

Mr. Kendrick smiled. "I'm aware of that."

Pumpkin had jumped down from Detective Pelley's lap and was patrolling the room, sniffing suspiciously at the yellow tape. He seemed particularly interested in one area, pawing at the papers on the floor and pushing them around with his nose. He finally sat down on top of them and yowled loudly.

"Come here, Pumpkin!" Kiki commanded. The cat didn't move. She knelt down and coaxed. But the big cat haughtily ignored her, staring off at the far wall as if he didn't know she was in the room. Kiki reached out to lift him from the pile of papers and Pumpkin hissed at her. Quickly, she dropped her hands.

She turned to look at the two men. "He doesn't do that to me very often," she said, "unless he has a good reason. I think he's trying to tell us something."

"What do you mean?" Detective Pelley asked.

Kiki hesitated. "Well," she explained, "sometimes Pumpkin acts like this to get my attention. It's like he wants me to know that he isn't just playing. That this is an important action on his part, and I should pay attention to what he's doing."

Mr. Kendrick smiled, and Kiki felt silly trying to explain.

"Sort of like ESP?" Detective Pelley asked.

"Sort of," said Kiki, brightening. "Once I lost a book, and he went out and sat in the glider on the back porch and wouldn't budge. The book turned up under the cushions on the glider. And he did it again last night, when he dug up the key in the flower bed. It was like he knew something was going to happen. Anyway, maybe that stack of papers has something to do with the break-ins."

"I had a dog once that could read my mind," said Detective Pelley. "I haven't thought of Jake in years. He got me out of some good scrapes!" He laughed. "Got me into a few, too."

"Well, I hardly think Pumpkin can solve our break-ins," Mr. Kendrick said. "But he's a great protector, Kiki!"

Kiki didn't say anything. Adults rarely understood what she meant when she told them about Pumpkin having a sixth sense. Not that she went around broadcasting it. She had told Andrew and he believed her, especially after the time Pumpkin had found his watch, exactly a week to the minute after he'd lost it. But even her mother, who was pretty cool about most things, brushed off the idea.

Kiki reached into her pocket for a chocolate bar and broke off a piece. She offered it to the cat, who had not moved.

"This'll do it," Mr. Kendrick said in a confidential tone to Detective Pelley. "This cat is a chocolate freak."

But Mr. Kendrick was wrong. Pumpkin looked at the piece of chocolate and shrieked so loudly that Kiki jumped. Then he went into a frantic dance, pawing the stack of papers until they flew in all directions.

"Pumpkin!" Kiki shouted. "Stop it!" She scurried around, collecting up the pages. The same heading was at the top of every page: *Superior Court 36251—Smith vs. Latham*. Kiki concentrated on the number as she stacked the papers in a pile. *Three-six-two-five-one. Smith versus Latham,* she repeated silently. She had to remember. She was sure that it was no accident that Pumpkin had messed up the file on this court case. No sooner had she started tidying things up in the wake of Pumpkin's tantrum than the cat slunk over to her backpack on the floor, and methodically, with amazing dexterity, started to empty it, pushing, prodding, and nosing at the books until they were all out on the floor. Then, with a grand huff, he walked into the empty bag.

"Strange surroundings, I guess," Kiki said, to explain her cat's behavior. The men were laughing at Pumpkin's antics.

"That's probably it." Mr. Kendrick leaned forward across the desk. "Kiki, I'm concerned about your involvement in this. Until I find out what these men are looking for, and until I'm sure that they can't identify you as the person who saw them, I want Detective Pelley to keep an eye on you."

"You mean like a bodyguard?" She made a face.

"Not conspicuously, but I'd like him to be around the school when you get there in the morning and when you leave in the afternoon. And he'll watch your house, too. It'll only be for a few days, I'm sure. I talked to your mother about it this morning, and she thinks it's a good idea."

"Mom's out of town today," Kiki said, frowning.

"I know. She's at the satellite clinic in Cloverdon."

"How did you know that?"

"Well, we *are* an investigative unit!" said Mr.

Kendrick, pretending to be insulted. "We have ways of getting information." He pushed his glasses up on his head. "It's just precautionary. Would that be okay with you?"

"Do I have a choice?"

"No, I guess you don't," said Mr. Kendrick.

Kiki nodded. "That's what I thought. Don't you have any clues in this case at all?"

"Not one."

Yeeeoooww!

Further conversation was cut off by a scream from inside the backpack. Pumpkin shot out of the bag like Halley's Comet, circled the room, and came to a screeching stop in front of Kiki. He looked up at her with pleading eyes.

"What's in your mouth, Pumpkin?" she asked, leaning over to take something that was hanging from between the cat's clenched teeth.

She stared at the piece of purple canvas and then handed it to Mr. Kendrick. "You have one clue now," she said slowly. "Pumpkin must have torn this off the man's shoe last night, and hidden it in my backpack."

Chapter Five

On the way back to school, Detective Pelley stopped at Burger Heaven and bought them each a double burger and shake. "You've missed your morning classes and your lunch hour," he reasoned, "and you have to eat. It's only fair that I treat you to lunch."

Pumpkin was sprawled on the floor of the car, contentedly licking the lid from Kiki's milkshake cup. When he was finished with hers, he pawed at Detective Pelley's leg until the detective relinquished his.

"You need to know, Kiki," said Detective Pelley, "that I won't be obtrusive. You probably won't even be aware that I'm around, so you don't have to worry about me embarrassing you in front of your boyfriends. Or girlfriends, for that matter."

"I don't have a boyfriend," said Kiki, blushing. "I mean, I have boy *friends*, like Andrew. But . . ."

"A pretty girl like you will have more boy-friends than you can handle before long. Do the guys a favor, though. Don't take Pumpkin along on your dates."

"Not if he acts like he did today," Kiki agreed, laughing.

Detective Pelley's voice became serious. "If I have to talk to you for some reason while you're at school, and somebody asks who I am, just tell them I'm your friend George. You can't go around calling me Detective Pelley without having somebody wonder why in the world Kiki Collier is talking to a detective."

"Okay," Kiki said.

"Now, do you have that number Mr. Kendrick gave you?"

"Yes, right here in my wallet with the other officer's number." She pulled a card out of her billfold and showed him.

"Good. If you ever need to use it, don't hesitate. That's a direct line to Lorne's office, and even if he isn't available, someone in that office will get a message to him. Okay?"

"Okay. But the police officer I talked to last night gave me a phone number, too."

"Well, since Lorne and I are now directly involved in this, I think you should call Lorne. If necessary, he can contact the police.

"And, Kiki, I want you to know that in ninety-five percent of the cases where I've had to tail someone, like I'm doing with you, nothing ever happens. Nothing. I don't think you're going to be threatened. We don't even know what those guys were after, but as Mr. Kendrick told you, he feels responsible because you were at his house . . . and because they saw you. Only briefly, I know, but they did see you."

Kiki's mind replayed that instant in the hall when the flashlight beam had flared on her. She decided not to say anything.

Detective Pelley put the key in the ignition and started the motor. "And just a reminder: don't talk to anyone about this."

"I've already told my mother and Andrew," Kiki said. "And Elena might have overheard me in the hall. I talked to Mr. Tanning, too, but I just told him that the house had been broken into while I was there."

"No prob. Just keep it quiet from here on. Any questions?"

Kiki lifted a snoring Pumpkin from the floor of the car and put him in her lap. "Just one. Can we drop this sleepy blob off at my house before we go back to school? It's time for his afternoon nap."

"Consider it done!"

* * *

There were only two periods left when Kiki got back—Home Ec and study hall. Mrs. Atkinson lectured on different kinds of stitchery and gave them a historical perspective on sewing that included a shocking story about young peasant girls in China who, years ago, went blind because they were forced to do intricate hand sewing with microscopic stitches on garments for rich people. The class was more interesting than usual—Kiki thought Home Ec was a drag unless they were cooking something or baking, both of which she loved to do. But her thoughts still revolved around her morning at the courthouse. She kept thinking about the papers Pumpkin had scattered and the piece of sneaker he had torn away. When the bell rang, she gathered her things and went directly upstairs to the *Courier* office.

The weekly paper was put to bed on Thursday and distributed on Friday, and she still had two stories to polish before the deadline. Andrew had assigned her to cover the girls' basketball team—that story was almost done, except for a few highlights from the last game—and she had to finish her profile on Ms. Montgomery, the school nurse. That would take longer, because Andrew insisted that any quotes used in a profile be verified by the interviewee. Then she had to do the layout and start on the pasteup, providing Elena was finished with her stupid column.

Kiki envied Elena, who by virtue of seniority had her own weekly column, "Morgan's Musings," in which she could write about any subject she chose. She did assignments, too, but never without complaining, and she was quick to let Andrew know when she was too busy to do something, such as edit a piece from one of their roving reporters or do a pasteup, because she was working on some smashingly creative piece.

When Kiki entered the office Elena was at the typewriter, intently gazing out the window, deep in thought. She typed a line, struck a pensive pose, and then typed another line. It was a posture Kiki had endured many times.

"Hi," Kiki said, not expecting an answer. She headed for her desk, noting with a private smile that the wastebaskets had been put back where they belonged. "Where's Andrew?"

Elena silenced the interruption with an impatient wave.

"Elena," Kiki repeated, "where's Andrew? I need to talk to him before I do a final on the basketball team."

Elena kept on typing until she was ready to talk.

"Sick," she said finally, without looking up.

"He went home. Flu. I'm in charge." She hit another key.

Kiki sighed. The only other time that Elena had been in charge, she had given Kiki a bad time about every article she had written—the lead was weak, the punctuation was wrong, the format was too busy, the headline stank. It was going to be a stressful afternoon, Kiki was sure. She pulled out her article on the school nurse and went down to Ms. Montgomery's office.

When she got back, Elena was still typing spasmodically. Kiki sharpened a couple of pencils, taking a little too long on each and watching with mild satisfaction as Elena registered irritation at the noise. Then she sat down to edit her copy.

Kiki thumbed through her notebook looking for the page on which she'd scribbled highlights from the previous week's basketball game. Nagle had been high scorer; Fernandez had had the most rebounds. The Pioneers had won by fourteen points. How could she expand that into two hundred words? She sighed loudly, leaned back, and looked around. Elena was still pecking at the typewriter, gazing into space, and pecking some more. Once in a while she would smile as if she was very pleased with what she was writing. Kiki scowled. She wished she could write a column. She'd write one about the court-house.

The dismissal bell rang, and the exuberance of three hundred students, give or take a few, seeped in through the closed door. She wondered if Detective Pelley would be out in front, watching for her, and what he would do if she didn't show up. She realized she should have told him that she sometimes had to stay late to work on the paper, especially on Wednesdays and Thursdays.

"Don't worry about me. Let me worry about you." That was what he'd said when she got out of the car, so she dismissed any guilt she had at not letting him know where she was. With Andrew out sick, she'd have to do layout and pasteup herself. Drudgery. She wished they had a computer that would do the layout for her. But there were no extra funds this year, Mr. Mucatti had said.

And she wished Andrew were here so she could tell him what had happened that morning. She didn't think Mr. Kendrick would mind that. Andrew could keep his mouth shut, and besides, he already knew what had happened the night before.

Kiki got up and walked to the window. The street was quiet. Only the stragglers were left—a couple of kids on bikes, and another trio horsing around as they walked to the corner. There was no sign of the green Dodge.

"Looking for Prince Charming on a white horse?" Elena asked sarcastically.

"Shut up, Elena," Kiki snapped without turning around. She could sense the older girl staring at her.

"My! Our irritability level is peaking out today," Elena continued.

Hot, unexplained tears clouded Kiki's eyes, and she wished she could come up with some biting remark to silence the girl behind her.

"Just finish your column," Kiki said, "or I'll be here all night doing the layout."

"I'm taking care of that," Elena said, her voice dripping with sweetness. "I'm going to do the layout *and* the pasteup for this edition. You can just leave it all in my very capable hands. Where's your sports story?"

Kiki wiped at her eyes with the back of her hand before turning around. What was the matter with her, anyway? This rush of emotion was strange, and she felt very tired.

"Where's the basketball story?" Elena demanded.

"It's almost done," Kiki said, moving back to her desk. She pulled the typewriter table toward her and sat down with her back to the other girl. In ten minutes she had finished the story. She rolled it out of the ancient machine and reread what she had written. Passable. Not great, but passable.

"Done?" asked Elena.

"Done," Kiki said. She walked over and put the piece in the final-copy box.

"Just run along," said Elena, sounding like Kiki's Aunt Miriam in one of her martyr moods. "I'll take care of it."

Scuzzball, Kiki thought. She gathered up her things. *Fine.* She'd *let* Elena do the whole thing. Then, feeling that she had to give some explanation, she said, "I don't feel well." It was true. She didn't feel well, but she didn't feel sick, either.

"Maybe you're getting what Andrew has," Elena said. Her voice held an uncharacteristic hint of sympathy, which only made Kiki feel more uncomfortable.

"Maybe," Kiki muttered.

"I'll have it ready to go to press right on schedule tomorrow," Elena continued. "Go home. Get some rest."

Kiki nodded. "Thanks," she mumbled, puzzlement shading her tone as she wondered at the reason for Elena's sudden generosity and, at the same time, not really caring. All she wanted to do was get home and go to bed.

She scanned the streets by the school as she stopped her bike at the intersection for the light.

If Detective Pelley was in the neighborhood, he was truly under cover. She began to wonder whether she'd dreamed the whole thing. Her head was feeling awfully light. Maybe none of this was happening; maybe the night before hadn't happened. Or that morning. Maybe Smith vs. Latham didn't exist. At this time the previous afternoon she had been sitting in The Sweete Shoppe with her friends Natalie and Jill, talking about Jill's plans to visit her sister in Florida over Christmas break. It seemed like twenty-four years ago, not twenty-four hours.

Kiki put her bike in the garage and went into the house through the side door. Pumpkin appeared and followed her to the kitchen, where she grabbed a soda from the refrigerator and penned a brief note for her mother: *I'm napping. See you at dinner.*

Her legs ached as she climbed the stairs. In her room she kicked off her shoes and flopped sideways on the bed, pulling the comforter up under her chin. Pumpkin burrowed in beside her, and within minutes they were both asleep.

When Kiki woke up, the room was dark. She lay quietly in the bed until her eyes became accustomed to the darkness and the frightening shapes around her transformed into familiar, unthreatening objects. The hunchbacked figure ready to leap metamorphosed into her fleece-lined denim jacket thrown carelessly over her desk chair; the slim, statuelike figure with wild hair by the window became her plant stand with a potted fern on top. Kiki curled her arm around Pumpkin, who was still sleeping, his comfortingly warm body rumbling as he rhythmically breathed in and out, in and out. She had no idea what time it was or how long she had slept, and she turned her head to squint at the fluorescent green numbers of the bedside alarm clock. Nine-twenty! She'd been sleeping for hours!

With effort, she swung her feet over the side of the bed and sat up. She still felt tired, and her whole body ached. Pumpkin's head poked up from under the rose-colored comforter, ears alert, green eyes watching. When she stood up to walk to the door he was into the hall before she was. The house was quiet, but a lamp from the living room splashed a pale yellow light over the foot of the stairs.

"Mom?" Kiki said as she padded downstairs in stocking feet.

"In here, honey."

Dr. Collier was sitting in the big lounge chair—the one they'd bought her dad for what turned out to be his last birthday—reading. She put down her book and smiled as Kiki came into the room. "Feeling better?"

"Yes and no," Kiki said, sitting on the footstool as her mother shifted her feet to make room. "Better, but not great."

"You look flushed," said Dr. Collier, reaching out to feel Kiki's forehead. "Did you take your temp?"

Kiki shook her head. "When I got home from school I just crashed." Pumpkin rubbed up against her legs sympathetically, and then jumped into her lap. "Sorry about dinner."

Dr. Collier laughed. "Don't be silly. I had some soup and a sandwich. Why don't I fix you some?"

"No, that's all right," said Kiki. "I'm not really hungry, just tired."

"Hmm, you may have picked up a flu bug. There's one going around."

"I know. Andrew went home sick this morning."

"Did Mr. Kendrick get hold of you?"

Kiki nodded. "It was an interesting morning, and that's an understatement." She told her mother about Pumpkin following her to school and acting weird in the district attorney's office. "I know you don't think he's really communicating when he acts so crazy, but I do. The only papers he touched were from the case of Smith versus Latham Superior Court."

Her mother leaned forward to stroke Pumpkin's long, silky fur. "The investigator cat," she said. She looked back at Kiki. "You know, your tiredness may be a reaction to all the excitement in the last twenty-four hours. I think you should go right back to bed and I'll bring you some tea and toast. You need to eat something."

"But Mom—" Kiki started to say.

"No buts, Kiki. It's two against one. Your doctor *and* your mother say, upstairs you go!"

Kiki sighed and stood up.

Her mother went on. "I'm still worried about this burglary business, especially with a detective assigned to you!"

Kiki rolled her eyes and snorted. "Mom! What is there to be afraid of? A couple of bumbling crooks break into a house, steal a cheap pearl necklace, and leave an antique opal ring sitting on the dresser, and everybody wants to make a federal case out of it. Come on! Whatever these guys were looking for, it wasn't me."

"Not a federal case," said Dr. Collier. "Maybe just a Superior Court case."

"Now you're making fun of me." Kiki could feel herself getting cranky.

"No," said her mother. "I just want you to admit your fear if you are afraid. Or, as our staff psychologist would say, don't stuff it!" Dr. Collier's bantering tone did nothing to make Kiki feel better.

"I'm not stuffing anything!" Kiki said, her voice rising. "And as for having a bodyguard out there, he was nowhere in sight when I left school. I could have been kidnapped three times and shipped off to Lebanon and nobody would have known!"

Dr. Collier ran her fingers through Kiki's curly red hair. "He was watching you, pet. But unobtrusively. Detective Pelley introduced himself to me when I got home from work. He was parked around the corner."

"Well, I didn't see him," Kiki mumbled. "I think I'll go back to bed now." She picked up Pumpkin and rubbed her face against his fur. "Sorry, Mom. I'm just grouchy tonight."

"That's okay. There's been a lot happening lately." She touched Kiki's forehead again. "You feel a little feverish. Take a couple of aspirins before you go to bed."

Kiki didn't even read when she got into bed. She drank a little of the tea her mother brought her, then curled up into a ball with Pumpkin on the pillow next to her, and fell into a fitful sleep.

Chapter Six

Kiki woke up the next morning with a splitting headache. Gingerly she lifted her head a few inches off the pillow and then eased it back down. Pumpkin, from a vantage point on top of the bookcase, stared at her sympathetically. The bedroom door opened and her mother came in.

"I guess I forgot to set my alarm," Kiki said, her head still down on the pillow and her eyes still closed. "What time is it?" She opened one eye and looked at her mother. She was dressed in her turquoise suit, Kiki's favorite, but today it seemed brighter than usual.

"Eight-twenty," said Dr. Collier. "I called the school and told them you wouldn't be in today. Here, take these." She cradled Kiki's head in her arm, handed her a couple of aspirins, and helped her take a sip of water. "You'll be better off in bed today."

"Is that a professional opinion?"

"Professional and free," said Dr. Collier, grinning. "I called Mr. Kendrick's office, too, and told them you were ill and would be staying home. Would you like some toast?"

"No thanks. No toast. And I'm sure Detective Pelley's got better things to do today than hang around a junior high."

"Okay, Kiki. Oh, I forgot to tell you that Mrs. Kendrick called last night. She couldn't find your scarf." Dr. Collier paused at the door. "Don't leave the house. It's nasty out."

"Leave the house?" Kiki mumbled. "I'm not going to leave the bed."

"There's soup in the kitchen," said her mother, closing the door quietly.

A few minutes later Kiki heard the car pull out of the driveway. She rolled over. Pumpkin, activated by this fleeting sign of life, jumped from the bookcase to the bed and charged at the drowsy girl, butting several times into her curled-up legs with his head, as if to prod her into response.

"It's Pumpkin, the fearless bull," Kiki muttered, feeling behind her for the playful cat. "Go attack someone else, Ferdinand. I'm sleeping." Chastised, Pumpkin sat on the edge of the bed sulking for a few seconds, and then jumped down to find some mischief he could engage in by himself. Kiki dozed off.

When she woke up at noon, Pumpkin had totally emptied a dresser drawer she had left ajar, and the room was artfully decorated from the bookcase to the door with bras, panties, and socks.

"Oh, Pumpkin," said Kiki, sitting up and surveying the wreckage. "You bad cat!"

Heartened by this attention, the cat responded by leaping from the windowsill to the bed, meowing loudly. He pawed at her with his front left foot, demanding more personal consideration. Realizing that it was not immediately forthcoming, he changed his tactics. He jumped to the nightstand and batted with his paw at the touch-sensitive light that Kiki's Aunt Miriam had given her for Christmas. On, off, on, off, on, off. He looked very pleased with his performance until Kiki pushed him off the bed and stood up.

"You nitwit," she said.

Her headache was gone and, while she wasn't hungry, a faint gurgling in her stomach reminded her that she hadn't eaten since the previous day's lunch with Detective Pelley. She slipped her feet into her scuffs and went downstairs, with Pumpkin enthusiastically leading the way.

In the kitchen, Kiki poured herself a glass of apple juice and sat down at the kitchen table. Pumpkin jumped into her lap and hummed contentedly as she absent-mindedly stroked him, starting at the top of his head between the ears and ending at the tip of his bushy tail.

"Well, looks like you and I have the place to ourselves today," she said. "We'll get to watch some daytime TV and that new video Mom picked up, if she didn't return it, and . . . wow, I could go for this life. It feels like I'm really getting away with something! And Elena is back in the office doing the layout and pasteup! I don't know what caused her sudden rush of compassion, but I won't question it."

Pumpkin jumped off her lap and took up a sentry position on top of her backpack.

"Killjoy! Reminding me about that math assignment. I'm two behind now."

She walked over to the window and looked out into the backyard. A steady drizzle was falling, and the sky was a dreary gray. "It's a good day to be home. I wonder if Andrew went to school today. . . ."

She walked to the phone and dialed the Carlisles' number from memory. It rang three times before Andrew's familiar voice came on the line.

"Hi," said Kiki. "Infirmary Two calling Infirmary One."

"You, too?" Andrew asked.

"Me, too," Kiki said. She felt better just having someone to talk to. They compared symptoms and decided that whatever it was, they both had the same thing.

"Well, I'm sorry it got you, too," Andrew said. "*The Courier* will have to go out late."

"It'll be on time," Kiki said, giggling. "Ms. Morgan had a venom relapse yesterday afternoon and offered to do the layout and pasteup."

"Good! It's about time she quit staring creatively at the ceiling," Andrew said. "She hasn't done a pasteup this year!"

"I took her up on her offer pretty fast," Kiki said. "She didn't have time for second thoughts."

"I hope it's a decent edition. Are you going back tomorrow?"

"Probably," Kiki replied. "I never have anything that lasts more than twenty-four hours."

"Me, either," said Andrew. "I could have gone in this afternoon, but it didn't seem worth it. Besides, when my mother left for work this morning she was worried about me being able to keep food down."

"Can you?"

"I ordered a double pepperoni pizza that was delivered a half-hour ago. So far, so good," he said, laughing.

"You believe in testing to the limit, don't you? I'm not even up to dry toast yet!"

"Did you hear anything more about the break-in at the Kendricks'?"

"Oh, yes! Get comfortable. Do I have a story to tell you!"

Kiki talked for twenty minutes, telling him about her trip to the courthouse and about Detective Pelley, and about Pumpkin's behavior in the D.A.'s office. When she was through, she swore Andrew to silence.

"Not one word will pass my lips," he said seriously. "It would be interesting to know what the Smith versus Latham case is about." He paused. "I'm sure I've read about that somewhere. It sounds so familiar. You know how some things stick in your mind?"

Andrew was as much a reader as he was a writer. He read two newspapers every day, and not just the sports sections, like most of the guys Kiki knew. And he remembered details.

"You know," said Andrew, "I might be able to find out."

"How?"

"Private investigation," he replied smugly. "If your cat can do it, I can." Kiki could imagine him grinning. "My brother has a friend in law school. I could call and see if I could catch him at the frat house. Court records are public information."

"Right," said Kiki. "But if the case hasn't gone

to trial yet or is still under way, there won't be anything on record. Besides, when would we have time to go to the courthouse and find out anything?"

"*We* wouldn't," said Andrew pointedly. "You're sick. But *I* have until five-thirty, when my folks get home. What time does the courthouse close? Five?"

"Beats me."

"I'll find out. Talk to you later."

Kiki hung up the receiver and leaned back in her chair. Andrew was right. She didn't feel much like getting dressed and going out in the rain, as intriguing as a "private investigation" sounded. At least Andrew hadn't laughed at her when she told him how Pumpkin had zeroed in on the Smith vs. Latham file.

Pumpkin, who had been sitting at her feet quietly listening to her conversation, looked up at her quizzically. She pulled him up into her lap and hugged his roly-poly body. "You go on a diet next week, fat cat," she said. "I may even get you an exercise bike for your birthday."

Meeeeooowww. The cat's tone let her know that her suggestion was not exactly at the top of his gift list.

Kiki walked into the living room carrying the cat and thinking over what Andrew had said. "You know how some things stick in your mind?" She did. And something was stuck in her mind that she couldn't quite pull out. Something her mother had said. *Was it last night? Or this morning? It must have been this morning,* she thought. She remembered all too well the conversation they had had the night before, and how she had growled at the suggestion that she might be afraid. Apprehensive, maybe. But not afraid. At least she didn't think so. But if she wasn't, why had she come downstairs a while earlier and checked the front door to see if her mother had remembered to lock it? (She had.)

What had her mother said to her? Something about a scarf. And Mrs. Kendrick. Her mother had been at the bedroom door and said that Mrs. Kendrick had called to say she couldn't find Kiki's scarf. *What scarf?* Kiki puzzled.

"I wasn't wearing a scarf," she said out loud. "Why would she be looking for my scarf?" She put Pumpkin down.

Eeoow! The cat rubbed up against her legs.

Kiki walked swiftly to the kitchen phone, but there was no answer at the Kendricks'. She shook her head. The whole thing was like a gigantic puzzle with someone else holding half the pieces. She went back to the living room and turned on the television set. Pumpkin was sitting on top of the VCR, playing with the buttons.

The red light on the left told her that he had succeeded in turning it on.

"What's this sudden fascination with VCRs and videotapes?" Kiki asked, lifting him down. "Are you trying to tell me something?" He raced around the room in a circle and skidded to a stop in front of the bookcase that held the videotapes. He looked to be sure Kiki was paying attention to him, and then pawed at one until it fell out on the floor.

"No, no, no!" she said, replacing the tape on the shelf. "I've already seen all of those. We're going to watch the soaps. If you don't like it, you can go take a catnap!"

Pumpkin jumped into the big lounge chair and curled up.

"Not in that chair," said Kiki, lifting him out and putting him on the floor. "You go find a nice windowsill or a heat vent or a pillow. I'm sitting here!"

The cat stalked away indignantly and curled up in front of the fireplace.

"Great theatrics, Pumpkin," said Kiki, changing the channel. "You do a superb pouting act. Next stop, Broadway!"

The cat harrumphed and refused to look at her.

During the next commercial Kiki went to the kitchen for more apple juice. On her way, she stopped and tried the Kendricks' number again. No answer. Throughout the afternoon, she tried the number five or six times, and with each unsuccessful call, she became more agitated. Why did Mrs. Kendrick think she had left a scarf there? Kiki hadn't said anything about a scarf. Why was it important enough to call her mother about it? And why wasn't Mrs. Kendrick at home? She'd been gone for hours. Was something wrong? No, that couldn't be. Detective Pelley had said they were keeping watch on the Kendricks' house, too. Kiki looked at her watch, which said four-thirty. If the courthouse closed at five, Andrew only had another half-hour. She wondered if he had found anything on the Smith vs. Latham case.

She carried her juice back into the living room. Pumpkin had given up his spot in front of the fireplace and was back working at the video shelf. This time he had four cassettes out on the floor, and had capsized the rest of the row.

"Oh, Pumpkin!" she said disgustedly. "I might as well wait until you're through demolishing it, and then put them back." She turned on the TV, curled up in the big chair, and dozed off.

The ringing of the phone woke her. Kiki tripped over Pumpkin, who was also racing to the kitchen, and grabbed the receiver on the fourth ring, just before the answering machine cut in. It was Andrew.

"Andrew! Slow down!" said Kiki as he started to talk. She could tell he was excited because every so often his voice would crack and the pitch would get higher. "Slow down! The phone woke me . . . start again."

She sat in a kitchen chair with her knees propped up in front of her and listened intently as her friend talked.

"I told you Smith versus Latham sounded familiar!" Andrew said. "I knew I'd read about it! It was a civil case about four months ago, and because there was such a large sum of money involved, the papers covered it."

"How much money?" Kiki asked, waking up a little more. She pulled her sleep shirt down over her knees and tucked her feet under her to foil Pumpkin, who was jumping at her bare toes.

"Over a million dollars," Andrew said. "And some of the pieces fit. Like the guy's name. Didn't you say one of the burglars was named Leo?"

"Yes!" said Kiki, now wide awake and listening intently.

"This is what happened," Andrew continued. "It's all public record. An elderly lady named Abigail Latham died last year and willed all her money to her nephew, Leo Latham."

"Wrong Leo. With a million dollars, he doesn't have to spend his evenings breaking into houses and stealing twenty-dollar pearl necklaces," Kiki muttered.

"Shut up! Let me finish. Leo has a half-sister named Shirley Smith. Shirley took Leo to court, contesting the will, which was written many years ago when Leo was a teenager and Shirley hadn't even been born. Shirley said that Abigail had made a later will that gave all the money to her. She said Abigail disinherited Leo because Leo's had several brushes with the law. But nobody can find the new will or the attorney who drew it up."

"I don't get it," Kiki said, thinking back to a civics class she'd had. "If it's a civil case, why is the district attorney involved?"

"I think the briefs you saw were for the civil case, which Leo won. But Shirley didn't roll over and play dead. She hired a private investigator named Flaherty to find the new will."

"Did he?"

"I don't know for sure, but he must have been getting close, because Leo roughed him up one night and ransacked his car and apartment. And that's the case Mr. Kendrick is prosecuting now. The People versus Leo Latham. Leo's out on bail. He didn't have any trouble posting bond because he's got all of Abigail's money."

Kiki leaned over and scooped Pumpkin into her lap to discourage him from chewing on a dish towel hanging off the sink. "So Leo broke into Mr. Kendrick's house and office," she said, "thinking that not only might he be convicted for assault and battery, or breaking and entering, but that if the D.A. has the new will, he might lose his inheritance."

"That's how I figure it," said Andrew.

"I'm impressed! You really got a lot of information!"

"Well, my brother's friend really helped a lot," said Andrew, but Kiki could tell he was pleased by the compliment. "And when I got through at the courthouse, I went over to the newspaper and spent some time in the morgue reading what had been written about the civil case."

"So what's our next move?" Kiki asked.

Andrew laughed. "What do you mean, *our* next move? You're sick."

"No, I'm better," Kiki replied. "You're not going to do anything else on this case without me!"

"Okay, you win. I thought that on Saturday we could visit the apartment building where Abigail Latham lived. Someone there may know if she made out another will."

"I'll have to think up a story for my mother. I don't think she'll appreciate my new career as a private eye."

"Mine, either," said Andrew. "We could play tennis first. That won't set off any alarms here."

"Okay. Oh, Andrew! Something else is bugging me. When my mom left this morning, she said Mrs. Kendrick had called to say she couldn't find my scarf, like I had been looking for one that I left behind, or lost. But I wasn't even wearing a scarf on the night I stayed with Jeffrey. What do you make of that?"

"Beats me," said Andrew. "But I have a one-track mind. Let's put the Case of the Mysterious Scarf on hold until we solve the Case of the Missing Will. See you tomorrow."

"Right." Kiki hung up the phone and absent-mindedly scratched the top of Pumpkin's head. She wasn't exactly ready to dismiss her mother's comment as lightly as Andrew had, but she also couldn't make any sense out of it. After a while, she realized she was hungry.

When Dr. Collier got home at six-ten, Kiki had meatloaf, baked potatoes, and a big tossed salad ready to serve.

"Somebody's feeling better!" Dr. Collier said.

At dinner, Kiki quizzed her mother again about Mrs. Kendrick's phone call, but Dr. Collier couldn't elaborate. "She just said that she was sorry she couldn't find your scarf," she said with a shrug. "She was in a hurry. She and Jeffrey were leaving to go spend a long weekend with her sister. Call her on Monday and straighten it out."

"I will," said Kiki. "So that's why I couldn't get an answer at the house."

She did her math and English assignments and started to watch a movie on TV, but gave it up after dozing off twice. "I'm going to crash," she said to her mother. "I can't keep my eyes open."

"Big day tomorrow?"

"Sort of," Kiki said.

But she didn't realize just how big Friday was going to be.

Chapter Seven

The next morning Kiki checked in at the *Courier* office before going to her first class. Andrew was already in the office, his legs propped up on his desk, reading.

"Hi," said Kiki. She looked over at Elena's empty desk. "Where's Priscilla Pulitzer? Reassigned to Mongolia, I hope?"

Andrew smiled. "No chance. She's taking the pasteup down for Mrs. Foster to run off copies."

"What's the rush? I wanted to take another look at my interview with Montgomery."

"I read the file copy you left," Andrew said. "Looked fine to me. And if it makes you feel better, I didn't see the final, either. She was on her way down with it, looking very smug when I came in. This issue is Elena's baby." He swung his feet down and stood up at the window. "Is your bodyguard on duty this morning?"

"I think I saw him on the way over here."

"Good. Are we still on for tomorrow?"

"Definitely! See you at lunch. I have Tanning first period. Gotta go and turn in these assignments."

Kiki had gym the last period before lunch. By the time she had showered and changed, the line in the cafeteria stretched almost to the door.

"Hey, Kiki!"

She turned to see who was calling. Barry Johnson and two of his buddies were leaning against the wall, reading *The Courier* and laughing. He waved the paper at her. "It's the famous Basement Babysitter!" he yelled. Some other kids in the line laughed. Almost all of them had a copy of the school paper, easily recognizable because of the yellow paper.

"Ignore him," said Angela Baracheck. "That must have been awful for you. I would have been scared to death."

Kiki's eyebrows knitted together. "How did he find out?" she said, almost to herself. She looked at Angela. "For that matter, how did you find out?" But as she said the words she figured it out. Without speaking, Angela handed her a copy of *The Courier*. On the front page, under Elena's byline, was the headline "Sitter in Basement, House Robbed." Kiki bit at her lower lip. Now it was clear why Elena had wanted to do the layout and pasteup. She hadn't wanted Kiki to see her column until it was printed. And with both Kiki and Andrew out sick the day before, she had had a perfect opportunity!

"Don't worry about it," Angela said. "Everybody knows about Elena's poison pen."

But Kiki barely heard her. She bolted from the line and headed for the stairs leading to the *Courier* office. *That witch! How could she!* she fumed. She heard Andrew's voice before she even reached the top of the stairs.

"Responsible journalists don't pull stunts like this!"

His voice squeaked, the way it always did when he was excited or angry. Kiki yanked the door open. Andrew was standing behind his desk, facing Elena. His face was flushed and in his hand he gripped a sheaf of *Couriers*.

Elena was not backing down. "It *is* responsible!" she shouted at him. "I checked my facts. She was babysitting at the Kendricks'. The police did answer a call to that address that night, while she was there. And she *did* get locked in the basement!"

"Did Lambert see this before it went to press?"

"Ms. Lambert doesn't edit *my* column," Elena yelled. There was a hint of smugness in her voice. "It's not hard news. A column is opinion or observation too, you know."

"There's such a thing as slander. And libel," Andrew said.

"This column is fact," said Elena. Defiantly she tossed her long black hair over her shoulder and flounced out the door, almost pushing Kiki over as she left.

Andrew looked at Kiki. "Have you read this?" he asked.

"Only the headline."

"Read it," he said tersely. "I'm going to find Lambert." He slammed the door behind him, and Kiki sat down to read. Her knees felt rubbery and her hand shook as she held the paper, but it was comforting to know that Andrew was so solidly on her side. With no brothers or sisters, she'd never had anyone fight her battles for her before.

MORGAN'S MUSINGS
by Elena Morgan

Sitter in Basement, House
Robbed

For those of you who doubt it, I can assure you that babysitting can be an exciting occupation. Check it out with a certain female member of the *Courier* staff, who discovered on Tuesday night that child care involves more than reading Dr. Seuss books and passing out cookies.

The sitter was ably assisted by her monstrous mongrel feline (shades of Dick Whittington!), who had the temerity to lock her in the basement while he was romping through the kitchen with the sittee. Presumably the cat assumed the sitter's role until our reporter could rise to the occasion (that is, get back upstairs to the living quarters).

The two burglars were routed (but not apprehended) by the cat, and a police report indicates that losses were small. That may be true for loot taken, but this writer wonders about repeat business for the sitter, since the home and child of our county's new district attorney were those left in her care.

My guess is no callbacks. Any babysitter out there looking for a new customer?

Kiki twisted a lock of her hair nervously. Having Elena publicly poke fun at her was bad enough, but what about the confidentiality she had promised Detective Pelley? With three hundred copies of *The Courier* floating around the school, there was no way to keep her identity a secret. When classes let out there would be copies carelessly left at the pizza parlor and The Sweete Shoppe and who knew where else. Anyone could pick it up, and while she wasn't named, it wouldn't take a master sleuth to make a few inquiries and find out who the reporter-babysitter was. Leo Latham was already out on bail for assault and battery. If he was one of the burglars and thought she could identify him, she might be in danger! She could kill Elena, raven-black hair, perfect nose, and all!

Andrew was back in five minutes. She could

tell by his expression that his meeting with Ms. Lambert had not gone well.

"Well?" she asked.

Andrew sighed. "She said the column itself is, quote, within journalistic parameters. There is a judgment factor, but you can't un-ring the bell. Unquote. Meaning once it's out there, you can't take it back. And if you try, that would only keep it in the public eye."

"That's what I'm afraid of," Kiki said. "How public is it going to be? I promised Detective Pelley that I wouldn't talk to anyone about it, although he knows that you and Mom know. But now almost anyone could figure out it was me."

"I know. I'm feeling better about your body-guard now."

"Me, too."

The rest of the afternoon passed quickly. Most of the kids who talked to Kiki were aware of Elena's razor-sharp tongue and sympathized with Kiki, but in the back of her mind there remained a nagging worry about *The Courier* getting into the wrong hands.

On her way home she counted three copies lying in the street between the school and the house. *Elena should do a consciousness-raising piece about littering,* she thought grimly.

She let herself in through the side door and was cheerfully greeted by Pumpkin, who led her into the kitchen and meowed piteously in front of the cupboard where his food was kept. She glanced over at his empty dish. "Sorry, old fellow," she said, reaching in and pulling out a bag of high-protein cat food. "I guess you *have* been neglected through all this. And you don't even know that today you were immortalized in print."

She filled the dish with kibble and then reached into another cupboard for a bag of chocolate chips. Deliberately holding the cat away with her leg, she buried half a dozen chips in the cat food. Then she stood back.

The cat leaped at the dish. Kibble went flying across the shiny kitchen linoleum in all directions as Pumpkin located the prized chocolate chips. Kiki laughed as she watched. "Dessert first, again! I'm signing you up for Weight Watchers next week!" But the cat, intent on finding his treats, never even looked up.

"Okay," said Kiki. "While you're creating a new floor pattern here, I'm going to get my science homework done." She walked to the doorway to get her backpack, and double-checked to see that she had locked the door to the garage. She assumed that Detective Pelley was off duty now. Maybe she should call Mr. Kendrick and tell him about the *Courier* article. She fished around in her jacket pocket and found the card he had given her. The number was busy the first time, so she waited a few minutes and then pressed redial. After two rings a woman answered. "Mr. Kendrick, please," Kiki said.

"Who's calling?"

"Kiki Collier."

Almost immediately Mr. Kendrick was on the line. "Hi, Kiki," he said. "What's new?"

Quickly she told him about Elena and the *Courier* article.

"That's unfortunate," he said, "but I don't think it's cause for alarm. It's unlikely that the men who broke in would get a copy . . . While I've got you on the line, Susan wondered if you happened to see her exercise videotape around the house on Tuesday night. She thought she left it on top of the VCR in the living room."

"No, I wasn't in the living room. Pumpkin may have knocked it down, though. He's been using our cassettes as toys lately."

Mr. Kendrick laughed. "I'll check under the couch," he said. "Give my regards to Pumpkin. And Kiki, don't worry. Detective Pelley is still on the job."

Kiki debated momentarily whether or not she should tell him what Andrew had found out about the Smith vs. Latham case. She decided against it. Actually, she had no way of linking the house burglary with the inheritance suit.

And to say that Pumpkin had given her the clue by scattering the Smith vs. Latham papers in his office would only amuse him. She'd been the butt of enough teasing that day already. Then again, the man's name *had* been Leo in both cases—but there were a lot of Leos in the world. She finally decided it would be best to wait and see what she and Andrew could uncover the next day at the apartment building.

"Oh, by the way, Kiki," said Mr. Kendrick, "did you ever find your scarf? The one your friend came looking for?"

"What friend?" Kiki asked guardedly.

"Oh, let's see. Susan mentioned her name. Elaine, I think it was. She went to the house yesterday on her lunch hour. Said you'd left your scarf and you'd asked her to pick it up."

So that was how Elena had verified her facts! She had been snooping around at the Kendricks', asking questions.

"Was her name Elena?" Kiki asked.

"That's it," he said. "I knew Elaine wasn't quite right. Did you find it?"

"Yes," Kiki lied. "Thanks."

"Oh, good. Do me a favor, will you? Drop a copy of the school paper off at the house for me. Just put it under the mat. I'm going down to join Jeffrey and Susan at her sister's for the weekend. We'll be back Sunday night."

"Sure," said Kiki. "Did you find out anything from the purple fabric that Pumpkin tore off the burglar's shoe?"

"I have someone working on it, but there were hundreds of purple high-tops sold in this county. And he may not even have bought them in this area."

"Oh," said Kiki, trying to keep her disappointment from showing. "Well, have a good weekend." She hung up the receiver and stared into space.

She thought about calling Andrew to tell him about Elena and the scarf but decided against it. She could tell him the next day. Right now she wanted to get her science homework out of the way. She dug into her pack, but her fingers couldn't locate the familiar spiral-bound book. Annoyed, she upended the pack and dumped the contents on the floor. Pumpkin watched the operation with interest and, thinking it was a new game, bounded from his position across the floor to the pile of books, then over to the empty pack, where he snuggled in, purring at having the entire interior to himself for a change.

"Rats," Kiki said. She looked at the cat, whose head was poking out of the blue denim bag, curiously observing her. "Okay, Pumpkin, you get to go for a ride! I left my science book in the

Courier office. And the one day I don't have math, I brought that book home." Kiki pushed Pumpkin over to make room for the math textbook.

There was no sign of Detective Pelley as she pedaled back to the school. She was irritated with herself for forgetting the book, and not even Pumpkin, who was licking the back of her neck with his sandpaper tongue, could improve her disposition. When she arrived, there was more than the normal amount of activity around the bike rack for so late in the day. School had been out for a good ninety minutes.

"What's going on?" she asked another eighth-grader. "Mass detention?"

He grinned. "Almost. It's dress rehearsal for the play next week. Definitely involuntary on Friday afternoon."

"No wonder," said Kiki, smiling back. Elena had babbled on about the musical the week before until Kiki could have screamed. She had written two columns about it, and had talked Andrew and Kiki into buying tickets for one of the performances. "Everybody turns out for basketball," Elena had complained. "Why shouldn't everyone support the arts around here?"

As Kiki and Andrew knew, Elena had a personal interest in getting a big turnout. She had

116

one of the leading roles. But they had finally given in and bought the tickets. In view of that day's column, Kiki wished she hadn't.

"Is that the monstrous mongrel feline?" the boy asked, pointing at Pumpkin with a rolled-up copy of *The Courier*.

"That's him," Kiki said, locking up her bike.

"Nice to meet a celebrity," the boy said, riding off with his friends.

The rest of the campus was deserted. Kiki hurried around to the front of the school to see if the main doors were unlocked. If they weren't, she'd have to find a custodian. But she was in luck. She entered, and the heavy door closed behind her. The empty hallway smelled of chalk dust and, compared to the usual hubbub when students were there, was ominously silent.

She paused at the foot of the stairs and looked down the length of the first-floor hall. All the doors were closed—the offices, the classrooms, the nurse's room. It was spooky. Kiki shivered and started up the staircase, her footfalls echoing hollowly in the stairwell. She got to the first landing, and heard voices from the upper floor. One sounded familiar—and had a British accent! Her scalp prickled and a knot of fear rose in her throat. She froze. But Pumpkin wriggled from the bag on her back and galloped up the stairs. She heard his ample body hit the door with a thud. Then someone screamed. Elena! Kiki ran the last short flight. The *Courier* office door was open and a terrible commotion was erupting inside. Elena was still screaming and a man was shouting.

"It's that bloody cat! Get that beast off me!"

And Pumpkin was shrieking—that high-pitched, relentless screech that turned him from a tame house cat into a wild animal. Quickly, Kiki slipped the heavy denim bag from her shoulders to her hand. Grasping it by the shoulder straps, she crashed into the room, swinging it at face level as first one man and then another ran by her toward the stairs with Pumpkin in pursuit. Their footsteps thudded on the hall floor below as they ran to the front door and pushed it shut, leaving Pumpkin snarling inside.

Kiki hurried to the window. An old black truck was pulling away from the curb. Exhausted, she plopped into a chair and took a deep breath.

Elena was standing by her desk, in costume for the dress rehearsal. She was visibly frightened. "What did they want?" she asked in a faltering voice.

"Me!" Kiki snapped. "They were the men who robbed the Kendricks' house the other night.

Your 'responsible' column apparently had some off-campus circulation."

"But—" Elena protested.

"It was a stupid, brainless thing to do, and you really put me on the hot seat! I hope you're satisfied. Your idiotic column backfired, and you almost got yourself into a real mess!"

"You mean they thought I was you?" Elena said. "I don't look like you!"

Despite her racing pulse, Kiki managed a grin. "You don't even look like yourself, right now!"

Elena was dressed in a navy blue sailor suit, and her long black hair was coiled under a man's brown wig and topped off with a sailor hat. Her usually rosy cheeks were smeared with charcoal so that it looked like she had a two-day growth of beard.

"No, I guess I don't," she said, going to the mirror on the back of the door to inspect herself. "I look terrible." Her nose was smudged with black, and several streaks of charcoal trailed down her neck.

There was a thump on the half-open door, and Elena started as Pumpkin strode into the room. He glared at her as he walked by, and harrumphed as he sank into a heap by Kiki's feet.

"Thanks, friend," she said, stroking him.

"That could have been serious." Pumpkin's whole body hummed as she petted him.

"I don't get it," Elena said defensively. She was getting over her fright and becoming the investigative reporter again. "I come in here for a few minutes to change and they think I'm you. Why would they think that?"

"Because they didn't see me clearly the other night. It was dark."

"But why would they be coming after you? I thought they just wanted some stuff in the house."

"Because they thought I could identify them," said Kiki.

"Could you?"

"I can now."

"What do you think they were going to do?"

"Threaten me. Maybe buy me off. Who knows? What did they say to you?"

"One called me a smart-mouth . . . and the other one said, 'So here's the basement babysitter!'" Elena blushed under her makeup and lowered her eyes. "I guess I set myself up for that, didn't I? I'm sorry, Kiki. I never intended . . ." Her voice trailed off. "I'm really sorry."

Kiki hesitated. She had vented her anger, and although Elena usually never apologized for anything, she seemed sincere. "Okay," she mur-

mured. "Actually, the only one of us they can positively identify is Pumpkin, and I don't think they have the nerve to take him on again." Pumpkin rumbled his acknowledgment. "Hurry up and change, and I'll walk to the bike rack with you."

"Thanks. Do you think they'll come back?"

"No, not unless they're stupider than I think they are."

It was almost five when Kiki got home. Dr. Collier had left a message on the answering machine saying she'd be late, so Kiki fixed a sandwich and ate while she was doing her homework. She looked around for Detective Pelley on her way home, without success, and thought about calling Mr. Kendrick, but then remembered he was leaving town for the weekend. Elena had been sworn to silence, and Kiki was sure that this time she'd do what she was told.

At ten o'clock she fell into bed, exhausted, with Pumpkin curled up at her side.

Chapter Eight

Andrew skidded up to the Colliers' door at ten o'clock sharp on Saturday morning, slamming on his brakes with such force that Kiki heard the squeal of tires before he rang the bell.

"I'm going, Mom!" she yelled as she opened the door.

Dr. Collier came out from the kitchen. "Hello, Andrew! Are you feeling better?"

Andrew gave her a mock salute. "I'm healthy," he said.

"Good!" She turned to Kiki. "How long will you be gone?"

Kiki looked at Andrew for an answer. She was uncomfortable about deceiving her mother, and was relieved when he responded.

"We'll play a couple of sets of tennis, and then have some lunch, and maybe take in a movie. There's a new one at the Crest, if the lines aren't too long. I'd say four o'clock, max. But we'll bring the Pumpkin back before the movie."

"Sounds like a full day!" said Dr. Collier. "See you when I get home, then. I'm back in emergency from noon till nine. And, Kiki, be careful."

"I promise. As long as Pumpkin's with me, those goons will keep their distance. Don't worry." Pumpkin's head popped out of the backpack that also held her racket.

"That's quite a vote of confidence for me," Andrew grumbled, feigning hurt feelings.

"See, I have two protectors! Not to worry, Mom."

"Is your mother having a delayed reaction to the break-in at the Kendricks'?" Andrew asked as they pedaled past the neighborhood video store toward the city park, where the tennis courts were.

Kiki told him what had happened in the *Courier* office.

Andrew's expression turned serious. "Those guys are really determined, aren't they?"

"Considering Leo stands to lose a million bucks, I can understand why."

"Yeah, I guess so," Andrew agreed, steering his bike onto one of the trails that led to the tennis courts. "I hope we don't have to wait for a court. Maybe the weather will discourage the weekend players."

"Let's skip tennis," Kiki said. "I just want to

go straight to the apartment building where Mrs. Latham lived and see what we can find out."

"And gyp me out of a chance to get even with you? No way!" The Saturday before, Kiki had beaten Andrew two sets out of three. "Besides it's too early to go visiting. Most old people sleep late, don't they?"

"My grandmother's up at six every day," Kiki said.

"Hmm," said Andrew. But he was right about one thing. The cold, cloudy weather had discouraged most of the weekend tennis players. Only one court was in use; the other two were empty. They locked their bikes and Kiki looped a long piece of blue nylon rope around Pumpkin's collar, while Andrew tied the other end to a tree.

"There you go, fellow! Enough rope to have some room to run, but not enough to get into trouble. That'll give the squirrels a fighting chance." The week before, Pumpkin had treed two squirrels and threatened to join them in the upper branches before Kiki caught him.

They played two sets and split.

"Tie breaker?" Andrew asked, mopping his forehead.

"Next week," said Kiki. "My mind's not on tennis."

"Mine either," said Andrew. "But I smell like I should go home and shower before I go visiting anybody, especially people I don't know."

"Me, too," Kiki agreed. "Come over to the house when you're cleaned up. I'll make some sandwiches."

Her mother had already left for the hospital by the time Kiki got home. She showered and changed and had a plate of tuna salad sandwiches ready when Andrew rang the front doorbell.

"Do we take Pumpkin with us?" she asked, feeding the cat her last half-sandwich.

"Might be a good idea," Andrew said. "Old people usually like pets. He could be an ice-breaker. You know, get them talking about the nice kitty." The nice kitty purred his approval as he licked the last traces of tuna from Kiki's fingers. "Are we ready?"

"Ready," said Kiki. "Where is this place, anyhow?"

"On the other side of the park. Not all that far."

They followed the same route they had taken in the morning, veering off one street beyond the entrance to the park's tennis courts.

"Is this place like a convalescent home?"

"No," Andrew said. "I looked it up in the yellow pages. Chelsea Arms caters to rich retired people. They're all 'independent-living apartments.' " He changed his voice to sound like a radio announcer as he reeled off selling points from the ad. "The apartments come in different sizes. The higher the floor, the richer the owner. There's a fancy restaurant, and a game room, and a gym, and a pool. . . ."

"What floor did Abigail Latham live on?"

"Fifteenth. Nothing but the best!" Andrew braked and motioned for Kiki to stop. "There it is."

Across the street from them was an imposing building of glass and black marble. A doorman was at the curb helping a woman get into a taxi.

"I get the impression," said Andrew, "that riding up on a bike is not cool."

"Right. So we lock our bikes in the park racks and go in on foot."

"Right. *If* we can get in. Pumpkin will never make it past that doorman. Can you tuck him out of sight?"

"We might not make it, either," said Kiki nervously. "This place looks like a maximum-security facility to me." They locked their bikes and she pushed Pumpkin's head down into the bag and fastened the strap, making sure that he had ventilation. "Sorry, cat."

"We'll never know if we don't try. Let's go!"

"Wait till the doorman's busy," Kiki whispered as they crossed the street. She grabbed Andrew's arm. "There's another car pulling up!"

They watched as a long, white limousine pulled up to the curb and the doorman went to meet it. A small silver-haired woman carrying an apricot-colored poodle got out.

"Now!" said Andrew. He grabbed Kiki's hand and dragged her in through the glistening glass doors. The lobby was decorated with crimson carpet and white drapes, and a lounge area with easy chairs was off to the left. To the right, a bank of mailboxes, each with a call button and speaker, was set into the wall. An elevator alcove was farther down, at the head of a sloping walkway that led to an underground mall of exclusive shops.

"What now, coach?" Andrew whispered. "Here comes the chargé d'affaires, or the maître d', or the inner palace guard, or . . ." Kiki ignored him as she hastily scanned the mailboxes. Just as the doorman came alongside, Kiki pushed a button.

"Yes?" came a voice on the speaker.

"May I help you?" asked the doorman simultaneously.

Andrew looked from the doorman to Kiki and opened his mouth but nothing came out, for at that precise moment the silver-haired lady with the apricot poodle walked up behind them. The backpack on Kiki's shoulders wriggled threateningly. Andrew's eyes widened and he moved closer to Kiki's back to shield the moving backpack from view.

"Yes?" the voice on the speaker repeated. "Who is it?"

"Kathryn Kristine Collier," Kiki said to the speaker.

Her words were drowned out by the poodle, who was attempting to leap from his owner's arms to Kiki's back, yipping continuously as he lurched forward.

"Oh, criminy," Andrew muttered. "Nice doggie . . ." He put out his hand. The dog snapped at it.

The woman smiled at Andrew. "Adolph doesn't usually like men," she said. "He seems quite excited at seeing you."

"That's an understatement," Andrew mumbled.

"May I help you?" the doorman repeated pointedly.

"No thank you," said Kiki, flouncing off toward the elevators, with Pumpkin writhing in the backpack. "We're going up to see my aunt . . . my Aunt Millie. Come on, Andrew!"

"Millie Ostenbush?" said the silver-haired woman. "Why, we're going to the very same floor! You just come along with me!" She turned to the doorman. "That's all, thank you, Fred."

The doorman retreated as the woman herded Andrew and Kiki into the elevator. Andrew cast a wary glance at the poodle. The dog's teeth were bared and he was snarling. Kiki backed into a corner, hoping to hide the gyrations of the pack on her back.

"Here we are!" said the woman brightly. She rapped the snarling poodle on the head and looked up apologetically at Andrew. "I apologize for Adolph's behavior. I guess he doesn't like you after all. But don't take it personally. He doesn't like most men." She glanced at Kiki in the corner. "What's the matter with your girlfriend? Cat got her tongue?"

"Yes, ma'am," said Andrew, managing a weak smile.

"Millie's apartment is the first door on your right," the woman said, pointing. "Have a nice visit." She walked down the hall and disappeared around the corner.

Kiki collapsed on the carpeted floor in a fit of giggles as Pumpkin thumped and bumped around in the backpack. Andrew was leaning against the wall, laughing so hard he nearly choked.

"Who the heck is Aunt Millie?" he asked when his laughing spasm subsided.

"Just a name I picked off a mailbox. I was looking for someone on the fifteenth floor. I figured that most older people have some hearing loss, so if I mumbled my name it wouldn't matter. And because most old people don't have many visitors, they probably aren't going to deny admittance."

"Nice psychology," said Andrew. "It's a good thing you're not Jack the Ripper."

Kiki slipped a piece of chocolate into the backpack for Pumpkin, who seized the opportunity to dart from the pack and race up and down the long hallway, skidding to a stop in front of the first door on the right. Kiki grabbed him and stuffed him back in the pack. "Sometimes you're a royal pain," she said.

The massive white double doors with curved golden handles were imposing. Gold-plated digits spelling out 1510 were mounted above the entrance, and off to one side was a lighted buzzer. Kiki pushed the buzzer. Pumpkin lunged at her from within the pack, and Kiki reached over her shoulder and patted him.

"I hope she doesn't have a dog," Andrew whispered.

"A dog would have barked at the bell."

"The way this place is built, you wouldn't know if they were launching rockets in there! Ring again!"

But Kiki didn't have to. As Andrew spoke the doors slowly opened, revealing an enormous living room decorated in gold and white, with floor-to-ceiling windows. A short, plump elderly woman with blonde hair and a well-wrinkled face stood in front of them. She was dressed in gold lamé culottes with a matching mandarin-collared jacket and gold high heels.

"Well, don't just stand there! Come in!" she commanded in a gravelly voice. "Come in!"

Kiki stared. She had never seen a room so luxurious. It looked like a movie set. Andrew poked her in the back and she walked past the woman, still staring. Beyond the living room, which was dominated by a white grand piano, was a dining alcove with white and gold furnishings and a crystal chandelier. Kiki looked down at her blue jeans and wished she'd worn a skirt and sweater.

"You must be from the high school glee club," said the woman. She smiled at them, creating even deeper wrinkles in her round face.

"No, ma'am, we're—" Andrew started to say, but she cut him off.

"Let me guess," said the woman. "You're a contralto." She poked a finger in Kiki's shoulder. Pumpkin yipped, but the woman either didn't hear or didn't want to acknowledge that she had heard. "And you," she continued, turning to Andrew, "you are a basso profundo! I can tell just by looking at you!"

"No, ma'am . . ." His voice trailed off as she continued.

"I consider it a privilege to be able to support the arts in our schools, especially music. I don't give a dime to the visual arts, though. Those painters are so . . . well, you know, flaky." She said the word with distaste and curled her lip. "They slop a little paint on a canvas, stick a milk carton in the middle, and call it art. I could do better dragging a raccoon tail through tomato juice."

"Yes, ma'am," said Andrew, grinning broadly.

"But music! Music is different. Music is precise. Music is a skill as well as an art. Music requires talent, honed to perfection." Her plump hands moved as she talked, and Kiki watched, fascinated. She had gold bands set with diamonds on six fingers! "Practice makes perfect, that's what I used to tell my students. I taught voice for twenty-three years, and I was on the stage for ten years before that. I told my students, 'You have been given a talent. It is up to you to perfect it!' " She smiled again. "Come and sit down." She gestured to a white-and-gold brocade couch. "I'll get my checkbook."

"Mrs. Ostenbush," said Kiki, holding up her hand. "We—"

133

But Mrs. Ostenbush was already heading for another room.

"We might as well sit down," Andrew said, leading the way to the couch. He poked Kiki's arm. "How do we turn her off? This is like one of those battery commercials."

"Maybe she just has to run down," Kiki whispered. She set her backpack carefully on the floor beside the couch. A gurgling sound floated up from the bag, followed by a few plaintive meows. "Shhh," said Kiki, patting Pumpkin through the denim. "She's coming back. I don't dare let you out in this . . . this palace."

Mrs. Ostenbush walked to a white velvet tub chair opposite the couch and dropped into it. In one hand she held a checkbook with an embossed gold cover; in the other, a gold pen. "How much do you need for your next production?" she asked, waving the pen like a conductor's baton and smiling.

"Mrs. Ostenbush," Kiki said, "we didn't come for money."

Mrs. Ostenbush dropped the pen and stared. "You didn't come for money?" she repeated. "But that's ridiculous! Everybody who comes here comes for money!" She started counting off on her chubby fingers, and Kiki noticed with surprise that even her well-manicured fingernails were painted with gold polish. "Last week it was the junior symphony, and the week before that it was the parochial school band, and the week before that it was . . . oh dear, I can't remember. I'll have to look it up." She flipped a page in her check register and ran her finger down a column. "The week before that it was the Engineers' Fife and Bugle Corps." Her blue eyes stared discerningly at Kiki. "If you didn't come for money, why did you come?"

"We came for information," Andrew said. "We came to see if you knew Abigail Latham."

"Oh," said Mrs. Ostenbush, her eyes filling with tears. She groped in a pocket for a handkerchief. "Oh, dear, dear Abigail. How I miss her!" She blew her nose on a gold-edged linen square. "Abigail was my very best friend. We did everything together. Well, not quite everything, perhaps . . . excuse me, where is your book bag going?"

"Uh-oh," said Kiki quietly, getting up quickly to retrieve the bag, which was laboriously shuffling its way to the dining alcove. She stooped to pick it up and gave an urgent whispered command to the interior. "Pumpkin! Stop that!"

"Why, that's quite clever!" said Mrs. Ostenbush, heaving herself out of the chair with a great push. "An automated book bag! High technology is wonderful, isn't it? Except I'll confess that all these new gadgets intimidate me—

135

microwaves and VCRs and remote-control security systems." She reached for the pack's closure strap, and Pumpkin's front paws poked out on either side and grabbed her hand.

"Oh!" said Mrs. Ostenbush, pulling back in surprise. Pumpkin held on.

"Pumpkin! Stop it!" said Kiki. She tried to loosen his grip on the jeweled hand. "I apologize, Mrs. Ostenbush," Kiki continued. "It's not an automated bag. It's my cat. It's how I transport him. He's been cooped up in here for a long time and he's getting restless."

"Well, then, you must let him out of there!"

"But he doesn't behave well in strange places," Kiki explained. "I don't want him to damage anything."

"Why, there's nothing in here he can hurt!" said Mrs. Ostenbush, looking at Kiki as she might look at a bully beating up on a small child. "Let him out!" Her fingers struggled with the flap as Kiki's eyes swept the room. Crystal vases with arrangements of fresh yellow roses adorned the end tables; tiny, fragile figurines in blown glass sat on the coffee tables; antique china graced an open three-step étagère. The *pièce de résistance* was the chandelier over the dining table. Kiki shot a pleading look at Andrew, but it was too late.

"There!" said Mrs. Ostenbush, extracting

Pumpkin from the bag. "Why, he's gorgeous! Majestic!" She carried him to the chair, holding him carefully in her arms as she ponderously lowered herself. Pumpkin curled in the crook of her arm like a baby, purring, as Andrew and Kiki stared.

"And by what name is this regal fellow known?"

Kiki swallowed. She thought briefly of changing his name to fit the surroundings, but she couldn't think of anything appropriate. Prince? Precious?. . . "Pumpkin," she replied.

"Pumpkin," Mrs. Ostenbush repeated, rolling the word on her tongue. She arched one eyebrow. "Well, that wouldn't have been my first choice, had I been naming him, but it does show some flair—a step up from Kitty or Tabby." Pumpkin acknowledged her approval by licking her neck, and she responded with a husky alto giggle.

Kiki sat back down on the couch beside Andrew, unsure of what she should do next.

"You might introduce me to your friend, Kathryn Kristine," said Mrs. Ostenbush, fixing a blue-eyed stare on Kiki.

"Then you did hear my name when I buzzed from the lobby!" Kiki said, registering surprise.

"Of course I did. Wasn't I supposed to? Do

137

you think all older people are hard of hearing? What stereotypical nonsense!"

Embarrassed, Kiki looked at her feet, but the awkward moment was broken when Andrew stood up. "I'm Andrew Carlisle," he said, offering his hand, which Mrs. Ostenbush accepted after shifting Pumpkin to the other arm.

"You're a wise young man, Andrew Carlisle," she said, waving him back to the couch. "You know how to sit by and observe without always needing to offer a comment. That's commendable. The only other person I knew who possessed that trait was the late Mr. Ostenbush."

"Thank you," said Andrew, smothering a smile. Kiki's lips twitched, too. The thought occurred to her that Mr. Ostenbush probably hadn't had the opportunity to speak two consecutive sentences during their entire marriage.

"Now, tell me what you two young people want to know about Abigail Latham."

Kiki and Andrew exchanged glances.

"Well, we both work for the school newspaper," Kiki began. "And . . . and . . ." She grasped for a plausible reason.

"And Women's History Week is coming up," Andrew said, "and we want to do an article on a successful local businesswoman."

"But because it's history, she has to be from the past," Kiki added, fearing that Mrs.

Ostenbush would be offended that they hadn't selected her.

"Why did you come to me?" she asked, leaning forward and setting Pumpkin down on the thick white carpet.

"It was an accident," Kiki admitted. "We just wanted to find someone who lived on the same floor, because we thought there would be a good chance that you knew her. And then Pumpkin escaped and ran up and down the hall and stopped in front of your door. . . ."

"You must know that nothing is coincidence," Mrs. Ostenbush said. "I'm convinced that it was not by accident that you chose my intercom, nor was it by accident that Pumpkin ran to my door. Animals have a much better developed sense of instinct than we humans. He knew exactly what he was doing, didn't you, Pumpkin?" She looked around the room for the cat.

"Pumpkin!" yelled Kiki, her eyes settling on the crystal chandelier. "Get down this minute!" She marched to the dining alcove. Pumpkin squinted his eyes at her and hissed.

Mrs. Ostenbush gestured at Kiki. "Come back and sit down, dear. He can't hurt anything. He's just surveying his domain."

Pumpkin purred loudly and swung the chandelier gently from side to side. The crystal baguettes tinkled. Kiki scowled.

"He's a very heavy cat, Mrs. Ostenbush," Andrew said. "He could loosen the fixture and some night you might end up with chandelier in your soup."

The old woman's face wrinkled into a prize-winning smile. "Let me worry about that, Andrew."

The chandelier tinkled again, and Kiki could almost see an I-win-you-lose look on Pumpkin's face as she returned to the couch. "Will you tell us about Abigail Latham?" she asked.

"I will," said Mrs. Ostenbush. She pulled out her handkerchief and dabbed again at her eyes. "It would be a privilege to tell you about Abigail's story. It's hard to believe that she's been gone a year now." She looked over at Andrew and Kiki. "But get comfortable. Take off your shoes! Curl up your legs!"

Kiki looked askance at the brocade couch.

"It's just a couch, Kathryn Kristine! Do as you're told!" Mrs. Ostenbush kicked off her gold pumps and wiggled her toes before adjusting to a comfortable position in the velvet chair.

Kiki and Andrew obediently did as they were told and curled up on the couch.

"Now, this is Abigail's story . . ."

Chapter Nine

Mrs. Ostenbush burrowed down in the chair and gazed off into space. "Let's see," she said, furrowing her eyebrows. "I first met Abigail twenty-one years ago. That's right. I remember seeing her in the record shop I always went to. We hit it off right away, probably because we both loved music. Of course I didn't know at the time that she was buying country-and-Western albums—they were right next to the opera section at the back of the store—but I eventually came to like Johnny Cash. And she sat through a few operas with me—*La Traviata, The Marriage of Figaro, Tales of Hoffman* . . ." She stopped in midsentence and trilled a few bars in a surprisingly strong and true voice.

Andrew glanced at Kiki, who looked at Pumpkin, who swayed on his crystal perch, providing a tinkling accompaniment.

"We were good companions for each other. I was already widowed, and she was a single lady—had been all her life. One thing you can say about Abigail is that she knew her limitations. She knew she'd never make it in a partnership. Abigail liked to be the boss. And she didn't give two hoots about what people thought. She had an equal number of blue jeans and evening dresses, and nothing in between. Oh, I take that back. I think she bought a pants suit once to wear to an afternoon tea, but she didn't like it, so she gave up afternoon teas."

"She sounds a little eccentric," Kiki said.

"She was a *lot* eccentric!" Mrs. Ostenbush replied, smiling as she remembered her friend. "And very unpredictable. Anyway, when I decided to retire from teaching voice five years ago, I moved here and Abigail did, too, because she liked the building."

"Did she have any relatives?" Andrew asked.

"Yes, she had a younger brother. Let's see . . . his name was . . ." She snapped her fingers, and the chandelier swung back and forth. "Gustav! Gustav married often and not always well. Abigail was always bailing him out of some mess. And Gustav had two children—a boy, Leo, by his first wife, and a daughter, Shirley, about fifteen years later by his third or fourth wife. Poor little thing. Her daddy died before she was born. And that was all the family Abigail had. Leo must be in his mid-forties now, and Shirley must be about thirty. Shirley used to come to see Abigail before she and her family moved to Texas."

"What about Leo?" Kiki asked.

"Leo!" she said with a harrumph. "That no-good bum! He was always in trouble with the police! And he never even sent a Christmas card to his aunt. But then he called Abigail out of the blue about a year before she died, all friendly and nice, and asking about her health. He'd read in the paper that she'd bought a video systems company. Probably didn't even know she had money until then. But Abigail hardly gave him the time of day. She thought he was fishing for a job. And I can tell you, she was not about to give him one."

"This is an expensive place to live," Kiki said. "Did Mrs. Latham inherit her money?"

"Oh my goodness, no! She worked for every penny! Her parents died when she was very young."

"What did she work at?"

"She was a waitress."

"A waitress!" Andrew repeated, not able to keep the surprise from his voice. "A waitress couldn't afford a place like this!"

"Quite right," Mrs. Ostenbush said, unperturbed. "She waited tables in her early years. She lived frugally for a long time, invested her money wisely, and made a fortune."

"What did she invest in?"

"Oh, she diversified. She backed some stone bands in Great Britain." Mrs. Ostenbush fluttered her hand in the air.

"Stone bands?" Andrew asked, puzzled.

"Maybe I have the wrong term. I'm always doing that. You know, the loud ones with the guitars and the amplifiers."

"Rock bands," said Kiki with a giggle.

"Rock, stone . . . what does it matter? She made a lot of money off groups that made a lot of noise and wiggled. She also had money in a computer company and in an outfit that made gym equipment. Her latest venture was a legal video production company. They specialized in videotaped depositions for accident cases and things like that. Abigail was the exact opposite of me. She loved tinkering with new gadgets. She'd think nothing of spending a whole day just figuring out how something worked. Frankly, machinery frightens me. The day she brought her video camera over, I felt like she had a gun pointed at my larynx." She put her hand to her throat.

"I know how you feel," Kiki said. "I don't like cameras, either." She glanced up. Pumpkin had come down from the chandelier and was stalking up and down in front of the floor-to-ceiling windows, looking in vain for a windowsill.

"Pumpkin's the ham in our family. If there's a camera around, he'll strike a pose and squeal until somebody takes his picture."

"I knew an opera star like that," said Mrs. Ostenbush dryly, "but he wasn't nearly as photogenic as Pumpkin."

Hearing his name, the orange-haired cat ambled over to the blonde woman and stood on his hind feet with his front paws in her lap until she lifted him into the chair.

"I don't want to make you sad," Kiki said to Mrs. Ostenbush, "but could you tell us how Mrs. Latham died? Was she sick?"

"Sick?" Mrs. Ostenbush shouted. "Abigail wasn't sick a day in her life, except for some bad clams that we got one time at a beach party in Fiji, and one time when she was piloting a small plane over the Bahamas and ran into a hurricane—I think she lost her lunch that afternoon. No, Abigail was as healthy as a horse. She died right here in this building, downstairs by the pool. She had just finished her thirty laps. I'd gone into the sauna while she was swimming, and when I came out, there she was, dead in a deck chair by the pool. Her heart just stopped beating. Can't say as I blame it. Trying to keep up with a woman like Abigail for ninety-two years would tax anything to the limit." She shifted Pumpkin in her lap and pulled out her hanky. "She was a wonderful woman and a good friend," she said, delicately blowing her nose.

"Well, thank you for the information and for your time," said Kiki, reaching for her shoes.

"Oh, you can't go yet!" said Mrs. Ostenbush, abruptly launching herself and Pumpkin from the chair. "We haven't had tea, and it's almost four o'clock!" She bustled off through an arched doorway, with Pumpkin trotting along behind.

"Whew," said Andrew to Kiki. "What a story! But we don't have any more information about a possible second will than we did when we got here. Do you think we ought to come right out and ask her?"

Kiki stretched her legs out. "I don't know," she said. "To tell the truth, I feel rotten about lying to her."

"Half lying," said Andrew. "We do work for *The Courier*."

"Yes, but we misrepresented our reason for being here. I feel like we're pulling an Elena."

Andrew nodded. "I don't feel good about it, either."

"I'm going to tell her," said Kiki.

"Tell me what, Kathryn Kristine?"

Kiki jumped. The thick carpet masked all sounds of people moving in the room, and Mrs. Ostenbush was standing behind the couch,

146

holding a tray of lemonade and cookies. Andrew stood up, took the tray, and set it on the coffee table while Mrs. Ostenbush came around and settled herself in the chair.

"Mrs. Ostenbush, we didn't level with you about why we came," Kiki began. And over lemonade and chocolate chip cookies, she told Mrs. Ostenbush everything that had happened.

Mrs. Ostenbush listened attentively, nodding her head while Pumpkin delicately nibbled at the chocolate chips she held out for him. When Kiki was through, she leaned forward and patted her hand. "That was not a serious misrepresentation," she said. "Especially since you promised that detective confidentiality. And you do both work for your school paper, right?"

Andrew nodded.

"Your errors of omission are forgivable. What we must deal with now, however, is the matter of the second will."

"Do you know if one exists?" Kiki asked.

"Of course it does! I know Abigail didn't leave her money to Leo, that, that . . ." She paused, groping for the right word.

"Nerd?" Andrew offered.

"Nerd!" said Mrs. Ostenbush. "Thank you, Andrew. Abigail herself told me she was cutting him out. I must have been in Europe when Shirley took him to court. I didn't read a thing about

147

it. I just assumed Shirley got the money." She looked up sheepishly. "But then, sometimes I don't read anything in the newspaper but the theater page and the comics. Abigail tried to get me to read the stock pages, but I couldn't understand all those columns of tiny numbers with secret codes at the top."

"So you think there's a more recent will," said Andrew.

"I'm sure of it! The original will was written many years ago. It gave everything to Leo, because Shirley hadn't even been born. And besides, how could Abigail know what a *nerd* Leo would turn out to be? That Leo made a big mistake when he called Abigail to snoop around about her affairs. I think he said something about not living forever, and that just reminded Abigail that she'd neglected to make a new will. She told him flat out that she wasn't leaving him a dime, because of his illegal activities."

"Did he argue with her?" Kiki asked.

"You bet he did. He said that he'd take her to court and prove that she signed the new will under duress. Or he'd prove that she was incompetent."

"What did she say to that?"

Mrs. Ostenbush smiled. "She laughed at him. She told him that she didn't have to sign this will. That she'd come back from the grave to haunt him . . . in living color. What do you suppose she meant by that?"

"Who knows?" said Kiki with a shrug.

"Did you get any of Mrs. Latham's personal belongings when she died?" Kiki asked.

"Any of them?" Mrs. Ostenbush yelled. "I got all of them! Nobody wanted them! When they cleared out her apartment, the manager gave me six crates of papers and toys. Plus all her blue jeans and evening dresses, which I gave to charity."

"Toys?" said Andrew, looking perplexed.

"Oh, you know. Gadgets. Her microwave. That's in my kitchen. I use it to store towels and dishcloths. It's the perfect size for that. Never did figure out how to use it for cooking, and besides, my friend Lila says microwaves can be dangerous." She glanced over at Pumpkin, who was investigating the wall to the left of the couch.

"Pumpkin, come here!" Kiki said, starting to get up.

"No, no, no!" Mrs. Ostenbush said, gesturing for Kiki to sit down. "He knows what he's doing! He's looking for something! And he found it!" she said triumphantly. "Isn't he cute?"

"Cute like a dead lizard," muttered Kiki, staring as half a wall slid aside to reveal a giant entertainment center flanked by rows of shelves filled with records and books and videotapes. The cat surveyed the shelves for a moment and then went directly to the cassettes and started pawing at them, pulling them out. One by one, they toppled to the carpeted floor.

"He's had this passion for videos lately," Kiki said apologetically, getting up. "He pulled all our cassettes down yesterday." She put the videos back on the shelf and picked up the heavy cat, who resisted by wriggling and yowling.

"Those videotapes belonged to Abigail," said Mrs. Ostenbush, wiping the corner of her eye.

"That sliding wall is really neat," said Andrew. He walked over to the wall and got down on his hands and knees. "Where's the button that opens and closes it?"

Pumpkin sprang from Kiki's arms and lunged at the baseboard. Slowly the wall slid back into place to hide the shelves and TV screen from view, while Pumpkin sat up proudly, waiting to be commended for his mechanical finesse.

"Showoff," Andrew mumbled, finally locating the button.

"Mrs. Ostenbush," said Kiki, "do you think the second will might be in some of the papers you have? I know her lawyer should have had a copy, but just on the off chance . . ."

"There's a possibility, dear. As a matter of fact, Abigail's old lawyer died several months before she did, and though I know she had gotten herself a new lawyer—a nice young woman—I don't think Abigail had time to acquaint the lawyer with all her affairs before she died. We could take a look through Abigail's things, but we'll have to go downstairs. I put all the cartons in my storage unit in the basement." She stood up. "I'll get my keys."

They left Pumpkin in the apartment and rode the elevator nonstop to the lower level. "I didn't have the heart to go through the stuff after Abigail died," Mrs. Ostenbush explained, leading the way through a basement corridor lined with numbered and locked storage compartments.

"This one," said Mrs. Ostenbush, stopping in front of a unit. She unlocked the door. "Those are Abigail's," she said, pointing to six large boxes in a corner.

"Can we use that hand truck in the hall?" Kiki asked.

"Certainly!"

Andrew and Kiki loaded the boxes on the cart and wheeled it back to the elevator, with Mrs. Ostenbush clicking along behind them in her gold high heels. After pushing the button, they waited for a long time. Mrs. Ostenbush consulted her gold watch. "People are coming home after an afternoon out. We do need more elevators for rush-hour traffic," she said.

Finally the doors opened and Andrew wheeled the cart in, positioning himself at the back. The cart took up a lot of room. Kiki and Mrs. Ostenbush followed. "It will take forever to get to my floor," said Mrs. Ostenbush.

She was right. The elevator stopped at the first floor. The door slid open. Three women wedged themselves in, and a white-haired man hurried across the lobby, waving at them to wait. Kiki pushed the hold button. When the man got to the open doors, instead of being grateful, he squinted and peered inside. "Why can't you delivery people use the service elevator?" he snapped, frowning at Andrew, who was scrunched into the corner. "I'll report you to the management!" Several other people were coming toward the elevators as he spoke, and Kiki, still pressing the hold button, looked past the man for a moment. Suddenly she drew in her breath sharply.

"Oh, no," she said under her breath. "Here we go again."

"I'll wait for the next one!" the man said. "I don't have to ride with delivery—"

Before he finished his indignant statement, Kiki had removed her finger from the hold button and pressed the one to close the doors. A familiar lump of fear was rising in her throat, and she held her knees together to keep her legs from shaking. She didn't speak until they were safely back in apartment 1510.

"Just wheel the cart into the dining room, Andrew," Mrs. Ostenbush directed, pressing the switch that illuminated the chandelier, "and we can spread the papers out on the table."

Pumpkin appeared from under a chair and stalked around the cart, sniffing at each carton. "Do you want to cover the table?" Kiki asked, looking at the table's burnished gold-and-white surface.

"Oh, I suppose so," said Mrs. Ostenbush, going off to get a cloth.

"Andrew!" said Kiki as soon as Mrs. Ostenbush was out of hearing range. "They're here! I saw Shorty downstairs in the lobby while that guy was making a scene at the elevator."

"Are you sure?"

"Positive. I got a good look at him yesterday. He must have followed us here and been stopped by the doorman inside, so he couldn't follow us upstairs."

"But we got here hours ago!"

"I know. When I saw him a few minutes ago he was wearing a jacket with a Chelsea Arms patch on the pocket. He probably figured out a way to get in and steal the jacket or something."

"How would he know we were still here?" Andrew asked. He held up his hand to silence her before she could answer. "I know. Did you see one or two of them?"

"Just one."

"Then the other one is watching our bikes to see when we leave. They know we're still in the building, but they can't know which floor we're on."

"They have a good idea now," said Kiki, "if Shorty watched the elevator. It only stopped at three floors." She ticked them off on her fingers. "Seventh, tenth, and fifteenth."

"Did he see you?"

"I'm sure he did. Should we tell Mrs. O.?"

"No. She's pretty secure in here. We need to get through this stuff and get out. He'll leave when we leave."

"Here," said Mrs. Ostenbush, coming back into the room carrying a beautiful linen damask cloth. "We can cover the table with this old thing." Kiki stifled a grin as Mrs. Ostenbush heaved the "old thing" across the table toward Andrew, who grasped the other side and straightened it over the surface.

"Pick any box," he said.

"Let's start on that end," said Mrs. Ostenbush. "Then we can systematically work to the other end. Abigail would approve of that. She was very systematic in her business dealings."

Andrew hoisted the first box to the table and

opened it. It was full of papers and notebooks—receipts and ledgers, Kiki guessed. They examined each item carefully, but there was nothing that resembled a will. They repacked the contents and went on to the next box.

"She didn't throw anything away, did she?" Kiki said as they finished the fourth carton.

"Abigail was a saver," said Mrs. Ostenbush. "I suppose that's how she got rich. I never had to worry about things like that. Mr. Ostenbush used to say, 'Millie, you just keep on singing and let me take care of the money.' So I did. And he's been dead twenty-five years now, dear man, and I have more money than I know what to do with, thanks to his investments."

Andrew hoisted another box to the table. "This one's got rocks in it," he said, clunking it down.

"Oh, that's probably her toys," said Mrs. Ostenbush. "I don't think there'll be any papers in there, but we can look."

A loud buzzing interrupted her.

"What's that?" Andrew asked.

"Just the downstairs buzzer. Let it ring. I don't want to see anyone. They'll just think I'm not home."

The buzzer sounded again, followed by silence.

Kiki's heart was thumping. Had Shorty discovered which apartment they were in?

"Don't worry about it!" said Mrs. Ostenbush with a wave of her hand. "Let's get on with this. They can come back."

Kiki stripped the sealing tape off the top and opened the box. Pumpkin, now bored with prowling through the living room, came in to watch. He jumped up on a chair, then to the table, and poked his nose in the box.

"No papers," said Kiki, looking inside. "That looks like a CD player on the bottom, and there's a video camera, and some kind of kitchen appliance."

"That was an easy one," said Andrew, starting to close it up. "One to go." But as he was turning the top flaps in, Pumpkin jumped on the box, batting Andrew's hands away.

"Okay, big boy," said Andrew, pushing at him. "Outta here!"

"Pumpkin! Get down!" Kiki's voice was sharp. She was tired and worried and disappointed. It had been a longshot, going through Abigail Latham's things, but Kiki had really thought they had a chance of finding a will. And now they were almost at the end. If they didn't find it in the last box, they would be out of luck. "Get down, Pumpkin!" she repeated. Pumpkin hissed.

"You're getting real good at that," Kiki said crossly.

"Wait a minute," said Mrs. Ostenbush, moving toward the cat. "I think he's trying to tell us something."

Pumpkin purred and hopped off the box as Mrs. Ostenbush reached inside. She pulled out the electric grater and all its attachments, and then grasped the handle of the video camera.

"Wow!" said Andrew, looking admiringly at the camera. "That's top of the line! Can I look at it?"

Mrs. Ostenbush held it gingerly in two hands, as if it were going to explode before she relinquished possession. "Abigail said it was user-friendly, but she didn't convince me!"

"What a beaut!" said Andrew as he examined it. "Did you know there's still a tape in it?" He popped open the cassette door and removed the videotape.

Mrs. Ostenbush shrugged. "Abigail had hundreds of them," she said. "All cataloged."

"This one isn't labeled."

Pumpkin, who had been observing from a chair, suddenly let out a scream, bolted for the living room wall, and pushed the button. The wall slid back.

"He's really on fast forward today," Kiki said.

"He's telling us something," said Mrs.

Ostenbush. "But what?" Pumpkin punched a button on the TV and the screen filled with snow. "I think he wants us to play the tape," she said, holding up the cassette.

At the sight of the tape, Pumpkin's ears twitched nervously. His tongue flicked twice and his tail went up, the tip quivering.

"We're on the right track," said Kiki excitedly, looking at her cat. "That quivering tail is a signal. I've seen him do that before! Do you have a VCR?"

"Oh yes. Abigail gave me one for my birthday one year, but I never did figure out how to work it. It's on that shelf beside the screen. I'm not sure it's hooked up."

Kiki hurried across the room and checked the equipment. "It's hooked up," she said. "Give me the tape."

She turned on the VCR, popped in the tape, and pushed the play button. Pumpkin sidled over and rubbed up against her leg, purring. Then he sat on the carpet and stared at the screen. Mrs. Ostenbush and Andrew came in from the dining alcove.

The tape started to roll.

"This is the last will and testament of Abigail Gertrude Latham," said a woman's voice as an image floated to the screen.

"Oh, good heavens!" whispered Mrs.

Ostenbush, putting her hand over her mouth. "It's Abigail! In living color!"

She collapsed into the white chair and Pumpkin climbed into her lap, sympathetically licking her face as tears rolled down her cheeks.

Chapter Ten

"Who would have thought of a video-taped will?" said Andrew when the tape ended.

"Leo figured it out," said Kiki. "That's what he was looking for—a videotape! A will that didn't have to be signed, and was in living color!"

"That Abigail," said Mrs. Ostenbush. "I should have guessed that she'd use some sort of electronic gizmo." She was half laughing and half crying while she talked, and Pumpkin sat on her lap, studying her curiously. "Oh, it was so good to see her again!" She clapped her hands together dramatically, and Pumpkin jumped down. "Now, what are we going to do with it?"

"We're going to get it out of here," said Kiki.

Andrew looked up. "That may take some doing, with our friends in the building."

"What friends?" asked Mrs. Ostenbush.

"Coming back on the elevator, I saw one of

the men who broke into the Kendricks' house," Kiki explained. "We think they followed us."

"Oh dear," said Mrs. Ostenbush. "Do you suppose that was who rang from the lobby a while ago?"

"Probably," said Andrew. "Is there another door out of here besides the castle gates?" He gestured to the double front door.

Mrs. Ostenbush nodded.

"Wait! Before we do anything I want to make a phone call," Kiki said, digging in the pocket of her jeans for the card Mr. Kendrick had given her. "May I use your phone?"

"Certainly," said Mrs. Ostenbush. "There's one in the kitchen."

Andrew and Mrs. Ostenbush followed her to the kitchen, where Pumpkin had already positioned himself at a vantage point on top of the microwave.

Kiki dialed the number. The phone rang twice and a man answered.

"This is Daley," he said.

"I need to get a message to Detective Pelley," Kiki said.

"Who's speaking?"

"Kiki Collier."

"Hold a minute, please." There was a brief pause before he came back on the line.

"Yes, Miss Collier. Your message?"

162

"I know who broke into Mr. Kendrick's house and office."

The front doorbell chimed and Mrs. Ostenbush covered her mouth with her hand.

"The man's name is Leo Latham and he has a partner called Shorty. They were looking for a videotaped will. I have it."

The doorbell rang again, and Pumpkin vaulted from the top of the microwave and ran to the front door, howling.

"What is your location?" the man asked.

Kiki gave him Mrs. Ostenbush's address and apartment number.

"Are the suspects in the area?"

"Yes, at least one of them is."

"Don't leave the apartment. Keep the doors locked. I'll send a car right over."

"Thanks," Kiki said. She hung up the receiver.

"He's sending a car over," she told Andrew and Mrs. Ostenbush.

"I hope they hurry," said Andrew as the doorbell chimed again, sending the cat into a wild frenzy. "Where do you think Detective Pelley is?" He looked around the kitchen. "Does that door lead to the hallway?" he asked, pointing to a door at the end of the kitchen.

"It leads to a service hallway," Mrs. Ostenbush said, "where I leave my rubbish and laundry for pickup. There's also a service elevator that goes to the alley side of the building."

Pumpkin came huffing back into the kitchen and stalked over to the service door, prowling like a jungle cat ready to spring.

"Where could they be now?" Mrs. Ostenbush asked nervously.

As she spoke the speaker from the lobby crackled and a harsh voice came through the small grate in the wall.

"Listen carefully up there and do exactly what I tell you! We know you've got the will."

"It's Shorty!" Kiki whispered. "Hear the British accent?"

Andrew nodded and Pumpkin jumped at the speaker, hissing.

"Put the video outside the apartment door and you won't get hurt. I'm armed. Don't call the police or you'll regret it!"

Kiki looked at Andrew and Mrs. Ostenbush and shook her head. She reached over and pushed the speaker button.

"No way!" she said. "This tape's worth a million bucks and I'm not giving it up for nothing! I'll meet you in the lobby downstairs in five minutes. We'll negotiate."

Andrew frowned, and Mrs. Ostenbush gave her a startled look. Kiki motioned for them to be quiet and took her finger from the speaker button. There was silence for a few seconds, then Shorty came back on the speaker.

"Five minutes," he said, and the speaker went dead.

"No way are we going to open that front door," Kiki said to Andrew and Mrs. Ostenbush, who were both staring at her. "Let's go, Andrew! Out the back way!"

She tucked the cassette at the bottom of her backpack and stuffed Pumpkin in on top of it.

"Mrs. O.," said Kiki, "Lock the service door as soon as we leave and don't open it up for anyone. We'll phone you as soon as we've safely delivered the cassette to the police. Give me your phone number."

"Couldn't you just wait here until the police come?" Mrs. Ostenbush asked as she wrote down her number.

"We could, but I'm afraid Shorty will find the service door before the police get here. It's not nearly as secure as your front door."

"But what are you going to negotiate?" she asked.

"Nothing. We're not going near the lobby," said Kiki with a grin. "We're going to the alley and then to our bikes and then to the police. We'll try to lure them away from here as we go."

"Be careful," Mrs. Ostenbush said.

"We will. You lock this door behind us," said Andrew. "And don't open it for anybody!"

Andrew and Kiki stood in the hall until they heard the lock click. "Good," Kiki whispered. "She should be safe now until the police get here."

Andrew nodded appreciatively. "That's a good idea, luring Shorty away from the apartment! But what are we going to do with the goon watching the bikes?"

"Use our secret weapon," said Kiki.

Andrew smiled. "Pumpkin!"

"That's right! Neither one of them is particularly fond of him." The backpack heaved on her shoulders, and Andrew gave it a friendly swat.

The service elevator led to a hallway with a large door that opened into the alley beside Chelsea Arms. It was dark outside, and they hugged the building as they walked through the alley toward the street, stopping just short of the sidewalk.

"Wait here until the light turns green, and then make a run for it," Andrew whispered. He peered around the side of the building. "That guy is in the lobby waiting for us to get off the main elevator. But they'll both be watching the street—from opposite sides! Did you want me to take the pack?"

"Not yet. Pumpkin might get confused if we switch now."

"Okay, go!"

The two teenagers darted out of the alley and raced for the corner. They made it across the street just as the light changed and the traffic started up again. But Andrew had been right. The man in the lobby had seen them. He started to run. Horns blared and brakes squealed, and he retreated to wait for another green light. There was a shout from behind as they entered the park, and a shadowy figure by the bike rack moved toward them.

"Got your key ready?" Andrew whispered.

"In my hand!"

"I'll grab Pumpkin, and you get out of here with the cassette," Andrew said. "Ready?"

The approaching figure came out of the shadows. It was Leo! Andrew slipped his hands into the pack on Kiki's back and lifted the heavy cat out into his arms. Thudding footsteps approached from behind—the light had changed, and Shorty was bearing down on them. Clutching her key, Kiki headed for the bike rack.

"Hold it right there, little lady!" said Leo, moving to block her access. At that moment Andrew let go of Pumpkin. The cat sprang directly at the burglar's head, toppling him to the ground as the man used his arms to shield his face. Kiki yanked her bike from the rack and pedaled furiously out of the park, leaving a screeching, rolling mass of fur mauling the man on the ground. She looked over her shoulder. Andrew had his bike out of the rack and had mounted it, but he wasn't following. He circled around and disappeared into the trees in the park.

"She's getting away!" Shorty yelled. He grabbed a branch from the ground and flailed at Pumpkin as Leo rolled away from the screeching cat. He yanked his friend up. "Get the truck!" The two men ran for the street.

Andrew wheeled his bike back into the clearing and scooped a still-hissing Pumpkin up from the ground. "Good work, big boy!" he said, cuddling the cat in one arm. He pedaled hard in the direction Kiki had gone, and caught up with her three blocks from the park.

"We'll never make it to the house," he panted, looking behind him. "That's their truck coming now!"

As they approached a shopping center Kiki had a sudden idea. The grocery store and the beauty shop had closed for the evening, but the door of the video store was wide open. "Turn in!" she yelled. She skidded to a stop in front of the video store, abandoning her bike on the sidewalk in front. Andrew followed suit.

Kiki ran inside. The startled clerk looked up from behind the counter. "Hey! Where do you think you're going?" he yelled as she raced to the back of the store with Andrew, who was still carrying Pumpkin, hot on her heels. Outside, tires squealed and a loud engine sputtered into silence.

"Just passing through," said Kiki, stopping only briefly at a display at the back of the store before circling another rack.

"Hey! No pets in here!" shouted the clerk.

"Hold onto Pumpkin!" Kiki yelled to Andrew. "They're coming in!"

"What's going on? I'm calling the police!" said the clerk. The agitated man picked up the phone as the two burglars entered the store, just in time to hear his threat.

The men exchanged glances. "Gimme that bag!" Leo yelled, wrenching Kiki's backpack from her hand. "Let's get outta here! He's calling the cops!"

The two men ran back to the truck and, after a couple of false starts, the engine caught and they pulled away with a screech. Kiki leaned against the counter for support. Pumpkin, still in Andrew's arms, was straining to get down, angry at having been denied another chase. Kiki reached over and stroked him. "Calm down," she said soothingly. "It's all right. They're gone."

"It may be all right for you, but I'm still calling the police!" stammered the clerk, holding the phone in a shaky hand.

"Good," said Kiki. "Ask them to page Detective Pelley. He has a radio in his car."

The startled clerk stared at her. "Are you serious?"

"Dead serious," said Kiki, taking Pumpkin from Andrew. She nuzzled her face into his fur and whispered to him, trying to calm him.

"Detective Pelley, please," said the clerk, identifying himself and the location. He covered the mouthpiece. "He says Pelley's on special assignment," the clerk said to Kiki.

"That's right," said Kiki. "I'm his special assignment."

The clerk said something into the phone, then looked up again. "What's your name?"

"Kiki Collier."

He repeated Kiki's name into the phone and gave the location again before hanging up. "They'll try to reach him. If they can't, they'll send a squad car."

Andrew was leaning on the counter, looking morose. "All that for nothing," he muttered. "If I'd been just a little faster . . . if I'd only grabbed that pack out of his hand . . ."

"Not to worry," said Kiki. "They didn't get the tape!"

Andrew turned slowly and stared. "They didn't?"

Kiki shook her head. "No. Abigail's tape is safely stashed on a shelf back there. What they got was a copy of *The Pirates of Penzance*. While we were rocketing through the store, I switched tapes!" She set Pumpkin down on the floor.

Andrew started to laugh. "Wait till they find out! I hope they enjoy spending Saturday night at the movies with Gilbert and Sullivan! At least it's probably a better production than the one the Pioneer Glee Club put on last year! The least you could have done was get them a good flick—*Dick Tracy*, *The Godfather*, any Clint Eastwood movie . . ."

But the clerk wasn't laughing. "That Gilbert and Sullivan was a New Classics release," he said indignantly. "I'm holding you responsible for replacing it!" A crash from the back of the store interrupted him, and his eyes darted away. "What's going on back there now?" he asked in a nervous voice. There was another crash, and the clerk hurried out from behind the counter. "It's that cat!" he shouted. "That cat is destroying my displays! He's got videos out all over the floor!"

"Pumpkin!" Kiki yelled. "Come here!"

Pumpkin came flying out from behind a rack. He raced to the front of the store, past Kiki and

Andrew and the clerk, and flung himself right into the arms of the man entering the store.

"Detective Pelley!" Kiki said. "Boy, am I glad to see you!"

"That's the last thing I expected to hear you say after the runaround you gave me," he replied, trying to sound annoyed but failing. He put an arm around Kiki. "You're a hard one to keep an eye on!" He showed his badge to the clerk, and Kiki introduced him to Andrew. "I was doing all right," he said, grinning, "until the two of you split up at the bike rack in the park. At that point I was trying to watch four people and a cat, and you were all going in different directions! Now tell me what's happening."

Kiki gave him an abbreviated version of the afternoon's events, and then retrieved the tape of Abigail's will from the back of the store. "This is what they were after," she said, handing him the videotape.

"Good work, you two," said Detective Pelley. "I wouldn't ever want you working against me!" He paused. "But don't ever do a fool thing like playing detective again, do you hear? You could have been hurt! Those guys had a million dollars at stake!"

The clerk's eyes widened.

"It's time to get you home," said the detective. "We'll straighten up Pumpkin's mess first, while you preview Abigail," Kiki said, moving to the back of the store, where Andrew was already shelving videos. "There's a VCR over there."

Detective Pelley turned to the clerk. "May I?" he asked.

The clerk shrugged his shoulders. "Why not?" he said.

When he had watched the tape, Detective Pelley went back to the counter. "I'm taking the kids in my car and I'd like to store the two bicycles here until tomorrow. I'll sign a receipt for the video that was taken."

"Sure," said the flustered clerk. "Okay." He shoved a rental form at the detective, who signed it, still balancing Pumpkin on his shoulder.

"Come on, kids," said Detective Pelley. "Let's go."

"I'm wondering," said Andrew, climbing into the back seat, "what happens when those thugs look at the label and find out they have an operetta instead of the will? I'm thinking that if it was me, I'd go back to square one."

"Don't think," said Detective Pelley briskly, slipping the key into the ignition.

"Mrs. Ostenbush! They'll go back to Chelsea Arms!" Kiki yelled, jumping out and dashing back into the video store.

"Kiki!" yelled the detective. But Kiki didn't

stop. She picked up the phone and frantically punched in the numbers. After an agonizingly long thirty seconds she put down the phone and returned to the car.

"No answer," she said, slamming the door. "We've got to go back." But Kiki's comment wasn't necessary. Detective Pelley was already making a U-turn in the street and calling for a backup unit.

"There's the truck," Andrew said as they passed the park. "It's pulled up on the grass beside the bike racks."

Detective Pelley picked up his mike and gave the other unit the location of the truck. He was speaking quietly, but Kiki heard the warning: "Use caution. Suspects may be armed." *Mrs. Ostenbush is no match for those men*, Kiki thought. She shuddered, thinking what they might do if Mrs. Ostenbush couldn't produce the video.

Detective Pelley pulled up in a loading zone and jumped out. "You two stay here," he said sharply. But Kiki and Andrew and Pumpkin were right on his heels as he entered the building. He flashed his badge at the doorman, who, with a worried expression, pointed to the elevators. They rode in heavy silence to the fifteenth floor, and Kiki ran to the double doors in front of 1510. There was no answer when she rang.

"Around the corner and through that door," said Andrew, leading the way. "The service entrance! Hurry!"

Even in the dim light of the service hallway, the signs of forced entry were visible. The plywood door panel had been fractured and the door was ajar. Detective Pelley pulled out his gun and slowly pushed the door open with his foot, motioning for the teenagers to stay behind him. The kitchen was dark. They were halfway across the room when suddenly the overhead fluorescents flooded the room with white light.

"Oh, put that dreadful gun away," said a voice from the doorway.

"Mrs. Ostenbush!" Kiki yelled. "Are you all right? What happened?" She hurried to the woman and hugged her as Detective Pelley dashed across the kitchen and into the dining alcove.

"I'm just fine, dear," she said, "but the gentleman in the dining area is not feeling too well. I'm so glad you suggested putting a cloth on the table, Kathryn Kristine. He's made quite a mess." She looked over at Andrew and smiled a greeting. "Was that you who rang the bell just now?" Then she spotted Pumpkin. "Come to Millie," she said. The cat jumped into her arms and began to purr. She purred back. "You know, he purrs in the key of G. That's quite remarkable. Let's go into the other room. I'd like to meet your friend."

The teenagers followed her into the dining alcove, not knowing what to expect. Shorty was sprawled out on the floor there. An ice pack and a large Turkish towel splotched with bloodstains were under his head.

"Careful where you walk!" Mrs. Ostenbush cautioned.

The remains of the crystal chandelier lay in the middle of the table. Glittering in the white carpet were shards of glass.

"He insisted on searching through that box on the table. He was quite rude, actually, holding a gun on me with one hand and poking around in the box with the other. When I heard the creak I knew right away what was going to happen. And down it came!" She patted Pumpkin's head and scratched behind his ears. "I suppose I have you to thank for that, don't I?" she said, planting a kiss on the cat's head. "Maybe you should call for an ambulance. My phone isn't working," she said to Detective Pelley, who nodded and pulled out his radio. "You must be the policeman friend that Kathryn Kristine was telling me about."

He finished speaking, clicked off his radio, and smiled at Mrs. Ostenbush. "Detective

George Pelley, ma'am," he said, showing his badge.

"I'm very pleased to meet you. Would you like some coffee and chocolate cake?"

Pumpkin yowled his acceptance.

"He's still wearing those purple shoes," Kiki whispered, nudging Andrew as they watched the paramedics loading Shorty onto a gurney. "There's the place where Pumpkin ripped the fabric."

Pumpkin prowled around the cart, sniffing disdainfully until they wheeled it out to the hall and closed the door. Detective Pelley was interviewing Mrs. Ostenbush in the dining alcove and making notes as she talked, writing very quickly to keep up with the deluge of information she was offering him.

Finally, he closed his notebook. "Thank you, Mrs. Ostenbush," he said politely. "You've been a big help." He turned to Kiki and Andrew. "This time I'm really going to take you two home! The other unit has picked up Leo. He was waiting at the truck."

"Oh, you can't go yet!" said Mrs. Ostenbush. "You haven't had any chocolate cake! And now that I know how to operate that . . . that YCR . . ." She looked questioningly at Kiki.

"VCR," Kiki corrected.

"That VCR," said Mrs. Ostenbush, "I have this wonderful show that we can watch together." She hurried over and pushed the button, and the wall slid away to reveal the screen. "You know, that man was so belligerent when he came breaking in here—and he was an Englishman, too!—but you just can't tell about people. He slammed a cassette down on the table and said, 'You can keep this!' When I looked at it after his, uh, accident, it turned out to be one of my favorite operettas, *The Pirates of Penzance*! . . . Now, who would guess that a common criminal would appreciate Gilbert and Sullivan!" She popped the cassette into the slot and tapped a button, and music filled the room.

Pumpkin sat primly upright in front of the screen to watch.

"We really have to go, Mrs. Ostenbush," said Detective Pelley, apparently enjoying her enthusiasm. "But I think that, uh, Kathryn Kristine and Andrew would be happy to come back tomorrow and watch it with you. Right, kids?"

Kiki looked quizzically at Andrew and they both looked at Detective Pelley, who was grinning lopsidedly.

"Wonderful!" said Mrs. Ostenbush. "Come at three and we'll have chocolate cake."

Pumpkin yowled.

"We'll make it an afternoon at the theater!

And do bring Pumpkin. I'll buy him his very own cake. That's small tribute for the cat who saved my life! Come to think of it, though, chocolate mousse would be better for a cat than cake! *M-o-u-s-e*, get it?"

"Sounds purr-fect to me," said Detective Pelley, grinning at her. He winked at Kiki. "Pumpkin would make a great addition to the force. I think I'll suggest it to Kendrick."

"That was a dirty trick," Kiki said to Detective Pelley on the way home. "Setting us up for an operetta tomorrow."

"No worse than the one you played on me, getting yourself knee-deep in police business, Kathryn Kristine," he replied, giving her a pat on the shoulder. "Although even I have to admit that you and your orange furball were one step ahead of the police." He smiled. "Look at it this way: even investigative reporters need a cultural experience now and again!"

He hummed a melody from one of the operetta's songs all the way to Kiki's house, while Pumpkin purred an accompaniment from the back seat.

In the key of G.

402

GET READY FOR ABIGAIL, MELISSA, AND JULIA AND THEIR OUTRAGEOUS SCHEMES FOR SUCCESS!

Abigail just has to have a leather jacket. Julia needs new clothes, and Melissa dreams of writing books on a computer. But Abigail and her friends are broke until they decide to form The 3 p.m. Club and start up their first business!

__THE 3 P.M. CLUB #1: GET RICH QUICK! (OR TIE-DYE TRYING)
by Leslie McGuire $3.50/0-425-12968-3 (June)
What a great way to start a business—making tie-dye T-shirts. The T-shirts are a hit, but when Melissa's brother Walt gets into the picture, disaster strikes! Abigail has a major crush on Walt, but will the 3 p.m. Club's first business go out of business before he notices her? Can the girls turn things around before it's too late?

__THE 3 P.M. CLUB #2: MY HAIR TURNED GREEN (I FEEL BLUE)
by Leslie McGuire $3.50/0-425-12653 (August)
With their All Natural Beauty Salon, the girls can help the environment and make a little money, too. Besides, Melissa's determined to give herself a perm (her brother's friend, John, likes curly hair). But when Melissa's hair turns green the girls realize maybe they're in the wrong business.

One day Allie, Rosie, Becky and Julie saved a birthday party from becoming a complete disaster. The next day, the four best friends are running their own business...

by Carrie Austen

___ #1:   ALLIE'S WILD SURPRISE   0-425-12047-3/$2.75
___ #2:   JULIE'S BOY PROBLEM   0-425-12048-1/$2.75
___ #3:   BECKY'S SUPER SECRET   0-425-12131-3/$2.75
___ #4:   ROSIE'S POPULARITY PLAN   0-425-12169-0/$2.75
___ #5:   ALLIE'S BIG BREAK   0-425-12266-2/$2.75
___ #6:   JULIE'S DREAM DATE   0-425-12301-4/$2.75
___ #7:   BECKY BARTLETT,   0-425-12348-0/$ 2.75
          SUPERSTAR
___ #8:   ROSIE'S MYSTERY ON ICE   0-425-12440-1/$2.75
___ #9:   ALLIE'S PIZZA POOL PARTY   0-425-124686-X/$2.95
___ #10: JULIE'S OUTRAGEOUS IDEA   0-425-12552-1/$2.95